Night Before Dawn

Also by True Vine Publishing

Charge the Walls

I Hear God in my Head

His Beauty for My Ashes

Seasons Come

Dare I Ask, What Am I Afraid Of?

Holy Ghost Explosion

Journeys in the Spirit

Words of my Mouth, Meditations of my Heart

On Butterfly Wings

Deliverance

Seeds of Greatness

Life… My Teacher

Positive Thinking Changed My Life

24 Minute Ministry Family Devotional

He That Finds a Wife

Who Are the Many?

Night Before Dawn

A Novel

— Roschelle McKenzie —

True Vine Publishing Company
Nashville, TN

Night Before Dawn
Roschelle McKenzie
Copyright © 2008 by Roschelle McKenzie
ISBN—10: 0-9786088-2-8
ISBN—13: 978-0-9786088-2-8

Published by
True Vine Publishing Company
P.O. Box 22448
Nashville, TN 37202

All rights reserved. No part of this book may be reproduced in any form or by any electronic or mechanical means, including information storage and retrieval systems, without permission in writing from the publisher, except by a reviewer who may quote brief passages in a review.

Unless otherwise noted, all Scripture quotations are from the King James Version of the Bible.

Cover design by Michael Thompson
www.michaeldavidmedia.com

Back Cover photo by Kirk McKenzie

Printed in the United State of America—First Printing

To place orders for more books or get current information; contact us at www.TrueVinePublishing.org

Dedication

This novel is dedicated to my Best Friend, the Holy Spirit. You are the Author and Finisher of my faith and this book. Thank You for being my Counselor, Mentor and Confidant. I will love You until the end of time and into eternity.

"Praise the Lord. Praise the Lord. O my soul. While I live will I praise the Lord: I will sing praises unto my God while I have any being."

Psalm 146:1-2 (KJV)

Acknowledgements

Father, I praise You for who You are.
Jesus, You are the Lover of my soul.
Holy Spirit, I would be lost without You.

I thank You, Lord, for giving me the words and inspiration to birth this book. May You be glorified every time someone reads it.

To my mommy, *Rowena*: I thank you for exposing and grounding me in the Word of Truth. Thank you for your example of what motherhood looks like. Your children rise up and call you blessed! I love you.

Daddy- look at what God has done! I am so thankful for our renewed relationship, and that our latter days are greater than the past. I love you.

Ricky, Diana, Sasha and *Samantha*- I love you guys so much!

To the entire *Salmon Family*: I encourage you to keep your eyes upon Jesus, so that we will all be with Sheriff in Glory, when this old earth passes away. Much love to you and you are all in my prayers.

To my circle of sisters:

Toishi, my sister, my friend. How can I ever thank you enough for being there for me every step of our friendship? You have a very special place in my heart. "You my sistah, girl." I love you.

Ayana, we are truly cut from the same cloth. You are so special to me and I'm so grateful that our friendship has withstood every challenge and opposition. You're my sister for life.

Shana, my cousin, my sister, my friend. We've been together for so long, shared so many precious memories and have laughed until we ached. I'm glad that we're family, but more so that we're friends. I love you, girl!

Leah (Ayanna; whatever your name is), my friend and writing partner. Thank you for introducing me to True Vine. You are so full of talent and wisdom. Thank you for your prayers, wise counsel and encouragement. I love you.

Judine, Joel 2:28 is for you. The gifts, purposes and calling that God has blessed you with will not lie dormant in your spirit. God desires to use you. Up, you mighty woman of God!

Elaine, my dear sister. I so appreciate you for your consistent encouragement and "sister-ship". You have never allowed me to wallow in my discouragements when it came to writing this book. Thanks for pushing me to the limit, and thanks for your unending love and support. You are such a blessing. I love you.

Tia, (Herman) my girl! You are so dear to me and I thank you for always having a kind or encouraging word to lift my spirit. I love you.

Keshawn, I marvel at what God has done in you—you awesome woman of God! Thank you for speaking life to my spirit, encouraging and praying for me during the times when I was most weary. I love you for being you, and I am so blessed to call you my friend.

Cherlyn, my dear sister. What a special woman you are. Thank you for your giving spirit. May your baskets always be full. Thank you for your love, prayers and support. I appreciate and love you.

Jezel, my special sister. Thank you for praying for me and standing with me. You also, are such a special person, and I am grateful for your friendship. I love you dearly.

Valerie, my second mommy. Thank you for accepting and loving me like your own daughter. I'm so grateful for your unending support and prayers. I love you so much.

To the *Smith Family*, I thank you for your kindness and love, especially with No'ell. You have been there since day one! Thank you for your support. I am truly grateful.

I would like to extend special thanks to my Pastor and First Lady, *Leighton* and *Marjorie Smith*. Thank you for your uncompromising stance in the Word and commitment to the Kingdom of God. You both inspire me to "come up higher." Your ministry has impacted the nations. I also thank you for your continuous support, prayers and "stick-it-tivity." You are most appreciated.

A big "Bless Up" to all my FEM people! And a very special "Big Up" to the FEM Young Adult Ministry (Y.A.M.). Thank you all for your love, support and prayers.

Special thanks to *Jackie, Alethia, Rocky, Janet K., Sis. Iona, Kate G., Adeola, Jason* (keep dreaming; God will come through), and *Sis. Eartha*. Your encouragement and support during this process has meant more to me than you could ever know.

To my editors, *Basil Drummond, Anne Schulman* and *Shawn Haugen*: Thank you for sowing your time into my "baby." May God richly bless you!

To my publisher, *Timothy O. Bond*, and the *True Vine* team: Thank you for your ministry. It has given me the platform I need to share my talent with the world and to glorify God in the process. Thanks for your patience and encouragement throughout this entire course. May God bless you.

To my precious *No'ell*, my pride and joy. Thank you for bridging the gap. I love you, baby.

I've saved the best for last: My darling husband, *Kirk*. Thanks for believing in me, more than I have believed in myself. Thank you for pushing and encouraging me every step of getting this novel published. I love you so much, and I never want a day to pass without me reminding you. Thank you for loving me, and No'ell.

If I have missed anyone, please forgive me, and I truly thank and love you too.

I hope you all enjoy reading this book as much as I enjoyed writing it, and always remember that JESUS IS THE WINNER-MAN, ALL THE TIME!

Yours in Him,
Roschelle McKenzie

Prologue

I usually hated doing dishes, but this time was different. I took great pride as I washed each dish, cup and utensil, aiming to see my reflection in each one. I wanted Grandie's delicate China to be spotless as I scrubbed off the excess grease and residue left from Thanksgiving dinner.

My mind wandered far away as I gazed out the kitchen window into the backyard. It was long after eight o'clock, but the sky was still bright and sunny; it seemed like an early summer afternoon... *strange*. My mind wandered even farther.

I thought of the past, our childhood. I could hear the familiar sounds of our childish, joyous laughter to which we had been so accustomed. The days before all the bad stuff started happening, when life was still pure and innocence was all we knew. As short as that time was, I held on tightly to the memories. Oh, how I longed for those days...

As I drifted further in to sheer nostalgia, suddenly the sky opened. A radiant light emerged that was so blinding, yet irresistible; it hurt my eyes to stare, but I couldn't turn away. I had to place both my forearms above my eyes to alleviate the burden of the light on them. A Man who looked like the Son of God gloriously appeared.

It was Jesus!

I stood in total amazement, frozen by the intensity of what I was witnessing. His presence was immeasurably vast as the light that clothed Him shone more brilliantly as He drew closer. Dressed in garments of white, His hair was like wool, His eyes like flames of fire and His feet the color of bronze.

"Oh God, I'm not ready!" was all I could manage to say. "Jesus, I'm not ready, I need more time."

My heart was beating rapidly and forcefully. I fell to my face as though I were dead. The only time I looked up was when I heard the gentle, familiar sound of my brother's voice.

"Fear not."

I was no longer in the kitchen and my surroundings were indescribable. Bright whiteness was everywhere; it was like standing in the center of a massive high-wattage light bulb. Many emotions simultaneously invaded my soul. I was extremely excited, yet dreadfully fearful. Jumping to my feet, I saw him standing right next to the King of kings, Lord of lords, and without any thought I ran to embrace him.

"Melvin!" I screamed. "I thought I'd never see you again."

"Don't come any closer, Sabrina," he replied gently, holding his right hand out to stop me in my tracks.

"Do not be afraid, for I have come to urge you to prepare. If we are to meet again in Glory, you must let it go and be reconciled. Be at peace, Sabrina, and remember that the darkest part of a night is just before dawn."

After that declaration, Melvin and the Man began to slowly fade away.

"What does that mean?" my voice quivered at each word.

"Be at peace Sabrina, so we can be together again in Glory." And with that he was gone.

"Wait! Melvin, wait for me." I ran to try and grab hold of him, but to no avail. He was gone...

Then, at that moment I was suddenly back in the kitchen. Doom engulfed me like a thick layer of smoke. I felt the inner core of my soul tremble violently and my heart seemed to have shattered into a million fragments. I couldn't move. I couldn't even speak. I had *lost* him again. *How could he leave me like that?* I closed my eyes and screamed so loudly, that all the beautiful dishes I was cleaning broke, one by one.

"Sabrina! Sabrina! What is the matter with you?" I felt someone vigorously shaking me. I jumped up, startled, to find my fiancé Eric trying to wake me.

Oh God, it was only a dream.

Thank goodness it was only a dream. I grabbed Eric close to me like a desperate child yearning for a parent and cried like a baby.

Chapter 1

"Sabrina, it's eight o'clock. You are going to be late for work again today. Hilton is going to fire you if you're not careful," said Eric, trying to wake me by yanking the covers off.

"Mmm, leave me alone, I don't care. I don't feel good. I'm not going!" I groaned, as I snatched the thick, warm, Ralph Lauren down comforter back over my head.

"What's the matter Bri? Are you sick?" he inquired. I ignored him. After a few moments he continued. "Does this have anything to do with your episode last night? Do you want to talk about it?"

"No, Eric. Leave me alone! I don't want to talk about it. Just go-o-o!" I pleaded. I didn't want to hurt him, but I needed to be left alone.

I knew he was offended, because the next thing I heard was the bathroom door slam and the shower running. I felt bad. I knew he was trying to help, but no one could help me now. I felt sick, like there was a piercing pain in my heart. I just needed to lie there until whatever it was that was plaguing my spirit had been obliterated. I wanted to cry, but couldn't. I wanted to go in and apologize to Eric, but couldn't find the momentum. This gloom was heavy and unkind and something told me the only solution to remove its grip on my heart was to pray. But I was certainly not going to do that! Not now, not ever!

After what seemed like forever, Eric finally came out of the shower stark naked. I pretended to be asleep, because I knew how he was and what he expected whenever I stayed home from work. I couldn't even do *that* today! I saw him looking at me with desire and longing and it aggravated me even more. I watched him through the corner of my eye as he got dressed for work, and I thought to myself just how much I did love this man.

Eric Morrison was the finest man I ever knew. He stood six feet, six inches tall, with an amazing athletic body. He had the smoothest caramel complexion, with big, deep hazel eyes. He always kept his face and head clean-shaven, but whenever he grew it out, his hair had a soft wavy texture like that of a newborn baby. The minor oval scar, almost resembling a teardrop on the right side of his temple, only magnified the contour of his masculine face.

I was a lucky woman and I loved him dearly. He was also very good to me and I knew that I was very fortunate to have him in my life. Being Eric's woman made me forget about a lot of the pain and grief from my past. His love for me had become my mental, emotional and spiritual Novocain. Eric was my friend, lover and soul mate wrapped in one excellent package. Our wedding day was planned to take place in just eight short months and I would finally be married to the man of my dreams after dating him for five long, exciting years.

Everyone approved of our union. His sister Erica and I were very close, maybe more so than my girlfriend, Niqi, and I. His family had become mine and they loved me as their own; I even called his parents 'Mom' and 'Dad'. Eric and I were the perfect pair and becoming his bride would be the best thing that ever happened to me.

I was the envy of many women and loving it.

My man was sweet, successful and fine, so why do I feel so unhappy right now?

I've got to get myself together.

I started to doze off again when I felt his sweet lips kiss my cheek as he whispered, "Try to have a good day."

"We'll talk later, E. Okay? I promise." I said, holding the covers right by my mouth to prevent him from passing out from the pungency of my morning breath.

"All right, baby. I'll be home early so we can talk and sort some things out. Just try to have a good day."

Eric was always so understanding. Even when I would back away, he would give me room to breathe. Lately, I just have not been myself. I couldn't put my finger on the problem, but Eric was sensitive to my mental state and respected me enough to give me the space I needed. He was always giving of himself.

The moment I heard his car start and pull out of the driveway, I threw off the heavy blanket and turned over flat on my back to face the ceiling. Oh, how I wish this bed would swallow me up! I couldn't shake this gloom that consumed my heart.

What is wrong with me?

I lay there for a moment longer, staring blankly at the ceiling as though it would give me some insight or clue as to why I was so glum. The ring of the telephone startled me out of my trance and I hurriedly reached over.

"Hello," I answered, still trying to sound sleepy.

"What are you still doing home, Sabrina?" was the response that followed.

It was Hilton, my general manager at Banana Republic, sounding very annoyed.

"Oh, hi Hilton. I was just going to call you. I am really not feeling well this morning and ..."

"What else is new?" he interrupted. "This is the third time this month, Sabrina."

"No, really Hilton, I'm not well. I'm sorry I didn't call earlier. I was trying to make it," I lied, "but I'm just too weak to come in today. Can you just call whoever is on the on-call schedule?"

"Sabrina, I'm getting really tired of this irresponsible behavior. You are an assistant manager and I needed you here this morning. Do you realize that today is the Friday after Thanksgiving, the biggest shopping day of the year? The Christmas season is just around the corner, and you call in sick when I need you most! You are very unreliable, and I cannot depend on you."

"I'm sorry, Hilton."

"Yeah, well, I'm sorry too, Sabrina. You can come and clean out your locker and collect your paycheck when you *feel* better."

"You're firing me!" I exclaimed, but the dial tone was the only obvious answer to my question.

I quickly sat up in the bed in an effort to position myself to absorb what had just happened.

Oh, my God, I just lost my job. Hilton just fired me.

I had to mull it over in my brain until it made sense. I sat there completely numb for a minute until my eye caught the silver picture frame on the nightstand that held a photo of my twin brother, Mel. I glared at it with no movement or expression. Within seconds the memories that flooded my brain induced the tears that so desperately needed to flow. I moaned and cried for almost an hour, until the well of tears ran completely dry.

☽☾ • ☽☾ • ☽☾ ☽☾ • ☽☾ •

This is Eric Morrison. At the sound of the beep, please leave a message.

"Eric, are you there? Bri? Is anybody home? I'm just calling to..."

The answering machine startled me out of my emotional stupor and I hurried to catch it before the message being left was completed. I hadn't even heard the phone ring.

"Hello," I managed to answer, unable to conceal the pain and agony in my voice.

"Sabrina. What's wrong girl, you okay? Did something happen with Eric?" Monique asked dubiously.

"Hey, Niqi." I whined. "No, everything is fine with Eric. I'm just not doing well today at all. I miss Mel so much. I thought I was good, you know. But I guess since this is the first time I am without him for Thanksgiving it hurts that much more. No matter how hard I try, I still can't let go. It's just not right, you know. It's not fair."

"I know girl, I know. But you have to know that Mel is in a better place right now, and he's looking down on you, watching over you when you need an angel to watch your back. He's your guardian angel now, Sabrina. I wish I could say something to make you feel better," she replied, trying to console me.

"Thanks, Niq. I just want to get to that point where I don't have to hurt anymore. I want to get to the stage of acceptance and move on, but the minute I think I'm there, something happens to trigger the pain and the whole cycle starts again. I miss him and I still can't understand why *he* had to die. I just don't get it. That bullet should have hit my mother, not Mel."

There was a long pause. I knew Monique wanted to, but couldn't find the right words to ease my grief, so I decided to relieve her by changing the subject.

"And you know what else too, that idiot Hilton fired me today! Would you believe that?" I laughed, sniffling through the tears.

"*What?* What did you do?" she asked as she chuckled, quite amused by the situation.

I hissed my teeth. "Please girl, I don't even want to get into that. Thank goodness I've got a man with a job. Where are you?"

"Mid-town. You want to meet me for lunch? Since it's Friday, I'll take half the day off and we'll just hang out, okay?"

"Are you sure that Richard won't mind? No sense in both of us getting fired."

"Girl, I'm finished with my assignment for the January issue and have already started on February's. Believe me, with *Essential* and *Honey-Bee* practically begging me to join their team, Richard will give me gas and lunch money for the rest of the day. So, of course, he won't mind."

"All right, sounds good. I have some ideas for the wedding and I want your input. Do you want to meet at Scotch Bonnet at one o'clock?" I inquired.

She contemplated for a second before replying, "One o'clock? Um, okay, let's do it. See you later," she confirmed.

"Thanks for calling Niqi. I needed to hear your voice. I'll see you at one." I hung up the phone and prepared for my date with my best friend.

Chapter 2

It had been years since I last took the subway, and boy, had things drastically changed since then. Occasionally I rode the bus to work on bad snow days, but my car was my main means of transportation. Despite the fact that it was parked outside in Eric's driveway, I had the urge to ride the train today. It was obvious I hadn't recently taken this mode of transport and was a bit embarrassed when I asked to purchase a token. The station attendant looked at me as though I had two heads.

"Uh, you're joking, right?" the young woman scoffed.

"Excuse me," I retorted.

"You need to use the machine to get a Metro Card. We don't sell tokens anymore. Where you been?" she asked snidely.

What a witch.

I could see that not all things had changed for the better. New Yorkers will still be New Yorkers. I rolled my eyes and walked toward the kiosk that seemed to hold the only key for me to get on the train. I was completely bewildered as to how to use the Metro Card contraption. Then from among the many nearby observers, a young man of-

was her philosophy when it came to the opposite sex, but I never bought it.

Monique Henry was born and raised in Brooklyn, and lived on campus, free of charge, as partial compensation for the Resident Assistant position she held in Madison Hall. It was the same dormitory where I stayed.

At that time, I shared a double with a girl from Memphis, Tennessee, who was just impossible to get along with. Mallory Fenton was her name. Without any real cause known to me, the girl just didn't like me. In spite of that, I still tried to be cordial towards her, but my efforts only resulted in a rude, standoffish attitude. I had not been stranger to the pang of racism. I mean, I grew up in the South, but this girl was intolerably blatant. One day, I overheard her cackling on the phone saying: "it would have been better for them to put me to live with a bunch of monkeys than to live with this coon."

I was so heated when I walked in the room that day. I had had enough of her. When I dared her to repeat what she had said directly to my face, she played dumb and said that I misinterpreted what she was saying. She had the gall to tell me that I should have knocked before walking into my own room, so that I wouldn't run the risk of misunderstanding her remarks the next time.

Who did this girl think she was? I was so close to knocking her out, but I did not want to jeopardize my scholarship and run the risk of being shipped back to Georgia. That was the last thing I wanted to do. So I left it alone for the moment and decided to take it up with campus affairs. I made a report with Monique, who diligently sought the aid of the Resident Director.

A couple of days following the incident, they successfully moved me into a single room of my own. The school decided that they didn't want any negative publicity about tolerating racist students, so they didn't mind footing my bill for the single, for every semester until graduation, in exchange for my "cooperation."

Perhaps I should have been tougher about the whole thing, but at the time it seemed like a good deal and I just wanted the immediate gratification. I was satisfied with their terms and extremely grateful to Monique for sticking her neck out for me, especially because she had not known me that well. She said she always hated the way these "Redneck idiots came up North and behaved like their piss could make fruit juice." I thought that was funny. We had hit it off ever since.

It didn't take long to discover that we both had a lot in common: dysfunctional families and zeal to make it in this hard-knock life. I really admired her for all the barriers and challenges she had withstood to get where she was. She and her sister, Latoya had been in and out of group homes for most of their teenage years because the courts had declared their alcoholic mother unfit to care for them. They were both adopted by the System when Niqi was only twelve years old. None of their extended family members was willing to support them, so like many others, they soon became wards of the State of New York. Their mother died of alcohol poisoning a year later.

Niqi was determined to make lemonade from the lemons life hurled at her. Despite the harsh realities, both she and her sister made out well in their ambitious pursuits. Monique was granted a full financial aid scholarship to Columbia by the state, and successfully completed her Bachelor's degree in Journalism, achieving a Cum Laude Honor in the process. Soon after graduation, she landed a job as Chief Editor with one of the top magazines in publication. Toya got a diploma in Cosmetology from DeVry and two years later opened her own beauty salon in Park Slope. She called it *Comb Over Hair,* and the shop was always packed with beauty conscious women, eager to be the next in line for their touch-ups.

Not bad for two "social rejects" who chose to beat the odds and make something decent of their lives.

Niqi and I loved the same kind of music and movies, and had similar taste in fashion. She even liked museum hopping, and we made it a goal to check out at least one new exhibit each month. Like me, she never knew her daddy. He was killed by train in the subway when she was just a baby. Someone had apparently pushed him into the path of the oncoming locomotive, the D line to be exact. Whenever she talked about the incident, she called it the "D-eath" train. They never caught the culprit.

And my dad, well, he died before I was even born. That's pretty much all I ever knew about him. It was a taboo subject in my family and when they stopped talking, I stopped asking.

Niqi and I did everything that college girls do together. She always knew where the hottest party was and because of her I was able to explore and get to know New York as home. Even though I *used* to have a best friend back in Georgia, Monique's presence in my life quickly filled that slot. I never imagined sharing that best-friend title with anyone else besides Courtney Wallace, but within the first year of our acquaintance, Niqi aptly applied the label to our friendship and I just went along with the idea.

It wasn't until one Saturday night when she got an exclusive invitation to an industry party hosted by Cool Jams Records that our new relationship was born. Monique had had a lot of exposure to people in the industry because of her Journalism major. Many of her mid-term and final assignments consisted of meeting and interviewing various artists and producers in the entertainment industry. She had me so excited about going to this one event, and was convinced that we would meet and get contact numbers to the richest and best looking men in the business. I wouldn't say that Niqi was a groupie; she's my friend. But Monique had a way of being dogged about what she wanted and was resolute about getting it.

"First things first," she had said. "We have to go shopping."

Neiman Marcus was our first and only stop, and even though we didn't have the money to afford the Moschino and Versace dresses we bought, I still used the credit card Discover had the nerve to send me to make the purchases. At the rate we were going, price was not an object and we went all out. Besides, it was just a rental, and we planned to bring them back the next day.

The day of the event we went to Niqi's sister's salon, where Toya did our hair and makeup for free. We were really impressed with ourselves that night.

Niqi and I arrived at the party in a cab a little after midnight. The venue was in one of the elegant ballrooms of the Hilton Hotel in midtown Manhattan. Both of us walked in looking like poster girls for a high-class fashion designer. The party was packed with high rollers and GQ's all over the place.

We turned heads in every direction and it wasn't long before she and I were sitting at a table reserved for a private group, sipping fine champagne with some really fine men. Her expectations were progressively being met as each moment passed. The ambiance, the food, and conversation were charming and the gentlemen we mingled with constantly made sure we were comfortable. Unfortunately, the good life didn't last as long as we had anticipated.

Monique knew she shouldn't have been eating so much with the amount of alcohol she consumed, but the Italian-catered cuisine was irresistible. It didn't take long for her stomach to reject it all, because without any warning, she vomited all over herself, the table and me.

It was disgusting and extremely embarrassing. At that moment our table became the center of attention. The same guys who were initially adoring and admiring us so much, scornfully scurried away, frantically cleaning off any spatter of Monique's eruption that had spewed on them.

The two of us were way too drunk and mortified then to care about the dresses we had now *bought*. I pulled Niqi up by the arm and led her to the ladies' room. She was incoherent and totally out of it, moaning and groaning, suffering a sharp headache, the result of her inebriated condition. I tried my best to clean us both up, but the delicate paper towels that the hotel provided in the bathroom were not much use. It would have been better for us to have left to clean up at home. As we headed for the exit to catch a cab, one of the waiters came running after us.

"Who do you expect to clean that mess in there? You better act like you know," he angrily contended.

"Can't you see she's not feeling well?" I charged back at him. Where was the compassion?

"Well, you do it then. She's your friend, go clean that crap up."

He flung a damp dish towel at me and instructed that there was a bucket of warm water under the table. I couldn't believe this was happening. I looked at Niqi and saw how helpless she was. I helped her find a seat in the lobby and went to ask for an apron from that callous waiter.

In a state of pure humiliation, I shamefully went to clean up Monique's mess, the spectators contemptuously eyeballing me in the background. It was after that not-so-memorable night that she appropriately identified me as her "best friend."

⁂

The clamorous opening of the sliding door of my subway car abruptly interrupted my reminiscing of earlier days in New York. In stepped a young woman holding a Bible and some brochures in her hand. Her very presence alone commanded such attention that it caused me and other passengers to stop what we were doing to devote our attention to her. She was a pretty, well-dressed woman, around the same age as me, twenty-seven years or thereabout. She was about five feet three inches in height, but her poise seemed to give her a much taller stature.

As she strolled down the aisle, she handed out a small leaflet to each passenger. Some people shook their heads in refusal, but most accepted it so as not to seem rude. As she approached my seat, I saw that the information was literature about Jesus and I turned away in an effort to decline her offer. She tapped me on my shoulder, completely ignoring the indication that I was just not interested. I looked at her and she softly spoke.

"Please, just take it."

Annoyed by her pushiness and not wanting any further attention drawn to me, I snatched the paper from her grasp, put it in my bag, and silently hoped she would leave. Instead, the woman stationed herself in the middle of the car and began to speak in a forceful, clear voice.

"Behold, for the kingdom of heaven is at hand! He who has ears to hear, let him hear. The Bible," she said, while holding it up toward the ceiling of the car, "teaches that God loved the world so much that He sent His only Son to die for you and me, and if we believe in His name and accept His gift to us, we would have everlasting life. Do you know of that kind of love? It is wonderful, and extended to all who open their hearts to Jesus. I want to tell you firsthand that Jesus is real. He is not a myth, or a legend, or just a good prophet. He is God Almighty and wants to be real in your life; *if* you only open up and let Him in."

She turned to face the direction in which I was sitting and seemed to be staring directly at me. *How rude!* It felt so awkward for her to be gawking at me so closely, that I focused my attention away from her. She was less than concerned about my obvious uneasiness, because her attention remained fixed on me as she continued preaching.

"He is capable of healing you *wherever* you hurt. I know there are many of you who are hurting from deep emotional wounds of the past and present, and may feel that all hope is gone, but God is ready to restore every area of your life that is broken, but you must first invite Him to."

"Could you please take your Bible talk somewhere else!" yelled a man from the opposite end of the car. "I'm trying to read my paper!"

I silently agreed with him and internally applauded his effort to shut her down.

But she answered, "I'm sorry if you are being disturbed, sir, but there are people who not only want to hear this but also need to. So if you don't mind, I will continue to be about my Father's business."

I looked around the car, and noticed for the first time, a few people with tears in their eyes and some with their heads lowered in their hands.

"That's just it lady, I *do* mind!" the man persisted.

"God bless you, sir," she said and picked up again. "Jesus loves you just the way you..."

I had had enough of this gibberish and instead of moving to the next car, I decided to get off at the upcoming stop, for fear she might bring her sermon there. Since the train was already in the city, I decided to take a cab to the restaurant.

As the train pulled up to the next station, I bolted for the door, almost falling to my face as I tripped over the feet of the man who was sitting across from me. Mortified, I pulled myself together and proceeded to the opening doors.

"God bless you, my sister," said the preacher. I hissed through my teeth at her and swiftly moved out of the train and up the stairs toward the exit to the street.

Chapter 3

The weather had changed considerably from the time I left Eric's house. It was now very windy and a lot colder than before and I had to wrap my scarf and Shearling coat tightly around me. My hair blew in all different directions, stinging my face with every gust of air. It took a few minutes before I realized exactly where I had reached and was pleasantly surprised to see that I was only two blocks from Eric's office. It was only twelve fifteen and I still had forty-five minutes to spare before my lunch date with Monique. I opted to pop in for a quick visit while he was still on lunch.

I stopped to buy two bags of honey-roasted nuts from the peanut vendor on the street and put them in my coat pocket. They were Eric's favorite snack and he would appreciate them even more because they were fresh out the roaster. It had been awhile since I surprised him at the office and it would be a nice way to say I was sorry, especially after the way I behaved this morning. Seeing him would certainly make me feel better after the unnerving experience I had on the train. He was sure to get a kick out of that story.

I began to get so excited about seeing my honey that I could feel my legs making greater strides to get to his workplace.

As I turned the corner that led to the Corporate Building on Madison Avenue, I saw Niqi's SUV double parked in front with the hazard lights on. Strange.

What is she doing here? I thought to myself.

Then I saw them; Eric and Monique. My fiancé and my best friend. They stood on the passenger side of the vehicle as he held her close to him in an embrace that suggested that they were much more than pals.

I stopped in my tracks, cupped my mouth with both hands to keep from screaming and tried to get my brain to process what my eyes were beholding. My heart started to beat rapidly and I could feel my palms begin to get clammy despite the cold wind that hammered my body. I slowly backed up a couple of steps to the building on the corner of the street, surreptitiously putting myself out of sight, to see what was going on. He whispered something in her ear and she laughed teasingly at his comment. Oh how my heart ached! A million and one thoughts ran through my head.

What do I do? Do I just stand here? Do I confront them?

I wanted to run them both over with the peanut vendor's cart, but decided against it.

Instinctively, I reached into my purse for my cell phone and dialed Monique's number. Still watching them from the corner, I saw her gasp and point to the phone she already had in her hand. My name was displayed on the caller ID and Eric urged her to answer.

"Hey Bri," the backstabber answered, with a nervous tone in her voice. "Where are you?"

"The question is where are *you*, Monique?" I said, trying to hide my anger and distress.

"I'm still downtown. I'm just about ready to go over to the restaurant now. I should be there within twenty minutes. What's up?"

I snickered to myself.

'What's up?' she asks me. I wanted to scream, *"You tell me what's up, you tramp!"* But I held it together as best I could and replied, "Just come on. I'll see you in awhile."

I did not wait for a response and just hung up. I peered around the corner to see her explaining the phone call to him. He released her from his arms, kissed her tenderly on the mouth and walked her around to the driver's side. She climbed into the truck and wound her window down. She leaned over and he kissed her again. Then the vehicle took off.

My heart sank to the bottom of my soul and I felt faint. If it wasn't for the support of the building I leaned on, my knees were sure to give way. This couldn't be happening.

How could this have happened? When did this happen?

I stood there, frozen with shock and devastation, unable to make sense of what I had just seen. Where were the tears I needed to muster up at such a time as this? My head hurt so badly that I couldn't cry, even if I wanted to.

I stood there a few minutes more, passersby questioning if I was okay and needed any help. I wanted them to help me commit a double homicide, I thought, but I couldn't very well solicit that type of assistance, could I? With no verbal response or body language, they just assumed that I was either crazy or confused, and went about their own business.

With the sea of adrenaline storming inside of me, I decided to go after Eric. I followed him into the office building and saw him about to enter the elevator.

"Ma'am! Excuse me, Ma'am!" yelled the security guard at the front desk, "you have to sign in before you…"

I ignored him and kept going, hurriedly trying to catch up to Eric. The doors of the elevator closed just as I got there. Flustered and disappointed, I pushed all the elevator buttons, hoping for the next one to hurry and come down. I had no idea what I was going to do or say and I had just a few minutes to think. Nothing came to my mind. The right words would have to come at the time of confrontation.

I stepped off the elevator like a woman on a mission. The double doors to the lobby of Comstock Incorporated swung wide open as I thrust them aside in one shot. Janet Edwards, Eric's secretary, jumped back in her chair, startled by my audacious entrance. She was a plump, middle-aged woman with a very pleasant nature. Her glasses were perched firmly on the brim of her nose and she always peered over them whenever she spoke. I never understood that, but it worked for her. She had worked for Eric for a little over two years and he was very satisfied with her performance.

"Uh, hello, Miss Richards. Is everything okay? How can I help you?" Janet questioned me.

"Everything's peachy, Janet. I'm just going to pay Mr. Morrison a brief visit." I answered her, making my way toward the door that read: **Eric Morrison-** *Senior Financial Executive Director.*

"Mr. Morrison was just called into an urgent meeting with the Board Members."

I opened the door and turned to her. "Thank you, Janet. I'll wait here until he is through."

"They could be in there for hours, you know," she insisted.

She was annoying me. "I'll take my chances, Janet," I said curtly and closed the door before she had a chance to discourage me any further.

The entire office setting echoed Eric's persona. The Comstock Corporation was located on the seventeenth floor of the twenty-three-story building and Eric had a spectacular view of the Lower East Side of Manhattan and the East River. The large office was outfitted with all solid cherry wood furniture and in the middle of the room was a huge desk with a computer and a large leather chair in front of it. On the left side of the desk was a four-drawer cabinet, and on the right side a small table was attached.

The table made space for Eric's favorite gadgets: a palm pilot, company mobile phone and pager, and a Bloomberg computer that provided up-to-the-minute information on business and stock market news.

Above his door was a 32-inch-screen television, permanently set to a channel that produces and distributes financial market updates, breaking news headlines and even the weather. The volume was low, but the commentator's voice could still be heard if you paid close attention. I walked around the office confused and mystified, trying to absorb the predicament I was in.

Various wall spaces were decorated with his MBA degree from New York University, as well as certificates and awards from the various departments he worked in before moving up to the position he currently held.

On the wall opposite the certificates was a large framed picture of the department's *Financial Team*, all men, seated in the boardroom with Eric positioned at the head of the table. I had always liked that picture, but for the first time I noticed how arrogant he appeared. It was like looking at a complete stranger.

I looked away in disgust and to the right of his computer screen, my eyes caught a glimpse of a framed photograph of the two of us on our last vacation to Jamaica. It was a picture of the night he proposed to me. I picked it up and recalled how that trip was one of the best I had ever taken. It was there in Negril that Eric asked for my hand in marriage, only twelve short months ago. He had been so eccentric about it, but very romantic nonetheless. On our last night on the island, we had dinner at Rick's Café. I remember it so well.

The atmosphere was so serene. The sky's luminescence was incredibly amazing as the sun settled on the horizon of the island. Our maître d' seated us at a table outside the dining room, atop a 35-foot cliff that overlooked the ocean and the orange-reddish hue of the sunset beautifully reflected off the rocks and the seawater. It was the most breathtaking view I had ever seen.

A live band was in the center of the café and they played everything from slow reggae to smooth R&B. This was definitely the place to be and despite the hefty price tags, cost was never an issue for Eric. Our all-you-can-eat feast was made up of curried goat, peppered lobster tails, jerk chicken, rice and peas, a variety of steamed vegetables and a bottle of White Star Moet Champagne. During dessert, Eric had excused himself for the gentlemen's room and shortly thereafter the band began to play one of my all-time favorite songs, *Gotta Be* by Jagged Edge. The lead singer in the group did such a fabulous job on his version of the song. I wished Eric would hurry back so we could dance.

As I sat waiting for him to return, I was surprised to hear his voice over the microphone just after the song ended. I turned to see him standing on the platform with the band, asking everyone in the place for their attention.

"Excuse me, ladies and gentlemen. If I could please have your attention for just a moment. The last song the band just performed is dedicated to my girlfriend, Sabrina Richards." He paused for a second and then continued speaking, his undivided attention, and everyone else's, now focused on me.

"Bri, I have never met anyone who completes me the way you do and I can't see myself living without you. Jagged Edge said it best. 'I gotta be the one you touch, I gotta be the one you love; I gotta be the one you feel, I gotta be the one you need,' and if you'll have me, I want to spend the rest of my days filling your life with sunshine. Will you marry me?"

I sat at the table with my mouth wide open in total amazement, the tears streaming down my face. Eric made his way over to the table with a beautiful princess-cut, two carat diamond ring. He bent down on one knee and whispered, "Sabrina Michelle Richards, will you be my queen for life?"

My body was flooded with goose pimples. I placed my hands over my heart to keep from passing out as I whispered, "Yes, Eric Vincent Morrison. Yes, I will marry you."

He took my left hand, placed the gorgeous piece of jewelry on my finger, rose from bended knee, picked me up and began twirling me around and around. I had to stop him for fear I might lose my dinner all over him. The crowd cheered and applauded and the couple seated next to us picked up the camera that was on our table and captured that very special moment...

The tear that streaked down my cheek quickly brought me back to reality. I placed the photograph back on Eric's desk and plopped myself down in his big leather chair.

How could something that seemed so right, be so wrong?

This fiasco came out of nowhere. I would never have expected this; not from Eric! He had been my Prince Charming for so many years and I trusted him implicitly. This man was my lover and my best friend, along with Monique, and I thought our foundation was rock solid.

We had met about four years ago at Klub Elektric here in the City. I was a junior at Columbia and Niqi and I worked the bar on weekends. It was Eric's birthday and his friends decided to do something unconventional for him. Eric was a classy guy and although Elektric was an exclusive nightspot, his idea of a good time was going to the theatre, the opera and other formal affairs. His people reserved one of the VIP rooms in the club for a party of six, where Monique and I were bartending that night. She noticed him first and pointed him out to me.

"Check out the hottie in the leather pants," she directed, while drying a glass. "I think he's the birthday boy."

"Hmm, he is a cutie," I replied.

"See, that's the kind of guy I'm looking for. He doesn't look like your average boy toy around these parts; he looks like a real man. I think I'm going to personally deliver their next round," she continued.

I laughed. "Look at you, trying to steal Melinda's tips," I joked.

"No such thing. I'm just trying to be polite and hook a brother up for his special day."

She asked Melinda, the barmaid for this VIP room, for their next order, prepared it, and brought it over with a smile. Monique, however, was not smiling on the way back to the bar. In fact, she looked quite disturbed.

"What's wrong? What happened?" I inquired, partially amused.

She hissed her teeth. "Birthday boy over there wants me to give you this and he wants to know your name."

"Really!" I smiled big, but then quickly wiped it off my face, trying not to make her any more upset. "What did you tell him?" I asked, opening the folded napkin she handed me.

"I told him to ask you himself."

"You're not really upset, are you Niqi?" I asked, looking up at her.

"A little disappointed, but not really. Go for yours, girl. There's more where he came from." She winked at me and walked away.

Written on the piece of paper was his name and two phone numbers, one for his home and the other for his mobile. I looked up just in time to see him getting up from his table, making his way to the bar. Trying to look busy, I discreetly put the napkin in my apron and began wiping down the countertop.

"Hello, pretty lady," he began, as he sat on one of the barstools. "Can I buy you a drink?"

"Can you buy me a drink?" I echoed, amused by his approach. "I don't drink on the job, but thank you."

"What makes you think I meant right now?"

"Oh," was all I could mutter, a bit embarrassed. "Um… what do you want?"

"I'm glad you asked. Since it's my thirtieth birthday I'm hoping that you will give me exactly what I want."

"Oh, really," I said defensively, raising my hand to my hip. He had better not say something that was liable to get him a drink poured over his head. "And what exactly is that?"

He leaned over to the bar toward me and whispered, "I want your name and an opportunity to take you out sometime soon."

I was relieved. He was cute. Letting my resistance down a bit, I replied, "Well, happy birthday to you. My name is Sabrina, but my friends call me Bri. And if you have a pen, I'll give you my number and you can let me know when you're ready to take me out."

He excused himself to get a pen from his table. Within a minute he was back at the bar with his Blackberry. I recited my number and he typed it into his mini-computer. Then he took my hands and placed them in his.

"Well, Sabrina. It was indeed a great pleasure to make your acquaintance, and I look forward to getting to know you. I believe your friend already gave you my information, but my name is Eric, and you'll be hearing from me soon."

He kissed me on my hand and walked back to his table.

I blushed and turned around in time to see Monique watching me from the poorly lit entranceway to the employees' restroom. I smiled at her, but she walked away, unresponsive.

Eric called me two days later and the rest, as they say, is history.

And so was this sham of a relationship. I felt like such a fool. How did I miss this? Was I so blindly in love that I failed to notice the warning signs? There are always indications when your significant other is cheating and I somehow missed them. I should have been paying closer attention and taking notes when other women I knew had gone through drama with their men. What made me think I was exempt? Well, if Eric and Monique think that they're going to play me for a fool, they have another thing coming. I'm done with them both!

The time was now twenty minutes after one. Surely, Niqi had to be at Scotch Bonnet by now and was probably watching the door in anticipation of my arrival at any time. Too bad for her, I thought. Let her sit there and wait 'til she gets a cramp in her rear end.

Eric had been in his meeting for almost an hour now and there was no telling how much longer he would be. Janet did mention the possibility that I could be waiting for a long time. I wasn't going to wait any longer.

I began to search his drawers for some money for a cab and inadvertently opened the wrong filing cabinet. I came across some alphabetized folders and saw a file that had my last name and first initial on it. I didn't realize that Eric kept *"me"* in a file. I was taken aback. Curious to see the contents, I pulled it from its place and opened it. There were various receipts and account statements.

Nothing too damning here, I thought.

I attempted to put the file back, but then I glimpsed the infamous blue stationery from Tiffany's. For months I had been begging Eric to tell me how much he paid for my engagement ring and he was adamant about not telling me. All he would say was that he bought it at Tiffany's and it was worth every penny.

I know it was wrong to sneak a peek at this classified information, but then again, I'm not the one sneaking around with other men, and especially, not *his* best friend.

Fifteen thousand dollars! My eyes bulged at the sight of the figures. I looked down at my hand. Good Lord, he had spent a fortune on this ring. I knew it was expensive, but not to this magnitude. It didn't matter much now anyway, because it couldn't keep him faithful.

I closed the folder, put it away, and suddenly got an idea. I began to look to see if there was a file created for Monique. There were several files with the name Henry under the letter **H** in the cabinet, but only one with the initial **M** on it. It was evident that this folder was newer than the others were because there were no creases or marks on it. My heart was now racing much faster than normal. A strange fear struck me. Would the name in the folder read 'Michael' or 'Mark' or any other besides Monique's?

So much for wishful thinking because there it was, plain as day; **Monique Henry**. I began to feel the anger rise in me again as I viewed the materials in the file. Several printed e-mailed letters, a few cards, and even nude pictures of her!

I was repulsed. The last picture was fairly recent because it was dated September of this year. This affair had been going on for more than two months. I felt the blood drain from my face as I sat there in Eric's chair and silently wept. After the moment of despair subsided, I managed to get up and pull myself together.

I removed the file, closed the cabinet, and continued looking for some money. After finally finding the correct drawer, I took fifty dollars from a stack of roughly two hundred. I knew he wouldn't miss it. I picked up Monique's file and manipulated it to fit securely under my coat. Approaching the door, I quickly glanced in the mirror on the wall to make sure I put on the best face I possibly could at this time. I opened Eric's door and walked out of his office.

"Couldn't wait any longer, huh, Miss Richards?" uttered Janet as soon as she saw me. "I told you it would be awhile. Sometimes they spend the whole day in there."

"I know, Janet, you were right. Thank you for the warning, but I really didn't mind waiting. I do have an appointment and I can't wait any longer. Please, do me a favor. Don't tell Eric I came by to see him. I really want to surprise him another time when he's not so busy and I know he would anticipate my visit if he knew that I was here today. So can we keep this between us, Janet?" I proposed, hoping she would buy my fib.

She looked at me sympathetically. I wasn't altogether positive she believed me, but she looked over her glasses and said, "Sure, Miss Richards, I understand. I love surprises too, and I know Mr. Morrison would just love it."

I wondered if she knew. Had Monique been here before? I thought about asking, but didn't, fearing that I might give myself away.

"Thank you, Janet. I appreciate it; and you can call me, Sabrina."

"Enjoy the rest of your day, Sabrina, and I hope to see you on your next visit." I waved goodbye and walked to the elevator.

Glancing at my watch, I realized it was now twenty minutes to two and the city streets were a little less congested than they were earlier. Lunchtime was over and most pedestrians had returned to their offices. It was just as cold, but a lot less windy than before. I stood on the curb trying to flag down a cab and caught one within five minutes.

I needed someone to talk to. Someone who knew and understood me, somebody that could help me make sense of the hell I was going through. I thought of Erica. She was the perfect person and would know exactly what I should do. "132nd and Lenox, please," I instructed, as I entered the taxi. I opened my coat and pulled out the folder. Although eager to read its contents, I resolved to wait until later. Just then, it occurred to me how hungry I was. I hadn't eaten all day. I was famished. I suddenly remembered the peanuts I had bought earlier for Eric. I sat right there in the back of the cab and devoured both bags of nuts, while my mind mechanically replayed the series of events that had unfolded so far, step by step.

Chapter 4

As expected, Erica had not yet come home from work. She was an African-American Literature teacher at a private school for the more privileged kids in Manhattan. The school usually dismissed at three o'clock, but when she and Cameron had their daughter, she permanently dropped all of her eighth-period classes from her schedule. She was usually expected home at around two fifteen. I settled on waiting for her on the steps of their Harlem brownstone.

Erica and Cameron had been married for only two years. Their daughter Camille had been born one year prior. She was the cutest three-year-old you ever did meet, precocious and adorable. I was a bridesmaid at the wedding and Camille was the delightful flower girl. She was all everyone talked about, next to how beautiful the bride was, of course.

I really admired Erica. She was smart, sophisticated and regal. We hit it off without a hitch the first time we met. It was as if we had known each other forever. Our connection was the epitome of what sisters or sisters-in-law ought to be. The fact that we were both the sisters in a set of fraternal twins was the key ingredient that validated our relationship and made our bond so tight. She always said, "There is no better woman I could pick for Eric than Sabrina. He would be a fool to do anything to jeopardize what they have."

    I hated that I would be the bearer of bad news. She was bound to hit the fan when I told her he had cheated on me… and with Monique, of all people! It wasn't going to be pleasant to be the one disclosing that her brother was indeed the fool she feared.

    Erica had not liked Monique from the start and no matter how I tried to convince her to give the girl a chance, she would always say, "Bri, you had just better be careful with that girl. She has a bad spirit about her and I don't trust her. Just watch your back. That's all I'm saying." Now after all this time, I wish that I had listened to her.

    It had all started on the night of Erica and Cameron's engagement party. Monique and Erica were never formally introduced; they had only heard about each other through conversation. Erica had graciously extended an invitation for Niqi to attend.

    Mr. and Mrs. Morrison had reserved an oversized ballroom at the Green-Lakes Country Club to host the occasion. It was the perfect location to have a wedding, much less an engagement party. Overlooking the Long Island Sound on a starry summer night, this place was magnificent.

All of the two hundred guests that attended were dressed to the nines, the women in their designer gowns and cocktail dresses, the men suited up in the best tuxes and modish suits. Instead of a DJ, they hired a live band to entertain. The Karma Notes were made up of two keyboard and drum players, a bass, trumpet and violin player, and three singers. They performed genres from classic ballads to R&B soul. The group added a sophisticated flair to the already elegant affair.

The entire setting was literally golden. Several waiters floated around the room pouring expensive champagne from yellow-tinted bottles into the guests' empty golden goblets. The tapestries and wallpaper, down to the light fixtures, were all fashioned in highlights of gold.

Erica stole the show when she made her entrance, wearing a gorgeous Vera Wang long satin dress, and bejeweled Manolo Blahniks stilettos, which of course were colored all in gold. Her flawlessly pinned hair was styled in a bun, with a perfectly cut bang that left not even one hair out of place. Atop her lovely tresses lay a pretty gold tiara. It was all a bit extravagant, but I had to admit, tastefully done.

There was a photographer snapping shots of everyone and everything, and a videographer recording the entire evening.

"Say cheese!" instructed the photographer.

Niqi and I, hovered over the Sushi table, turned just in time to have our pictures snapped with mouthfuls of California rolls, marinated in Wasabi and soy sauce.

"Please take that one again," I pleaded realizing how ridiculous that photograph was going to look once it was developed.

"No," Erica interrupted, releasing the photographer to make his next move on another unsuspecting victim. "Those are the ones I'm going to cherish." She smiled at Niqi as she embraced me. She really did look stunning.

"You must be Monique." Erica extended her hand and they both exchanged pleasantries. "I've heard a lot about you. It's nice to finally put a face to a name."

"Same here. Bri talks about how great you are all the time. Thank you for inviting me to this very special occasion. You look wonderful," Niqi replied.

"Oh, this old thing," Erica said twirling, as the tail of her dress created a fanlike whirl mimicking her every move. We all laughed at her feigned modesty.

"You really do, Erica. Fabulous is the word I would use. Cameron must be bursting at the seams. Where is he anyway?" I asked looking around for his whereabouts.

"With your man, picking up my parents. They should be here any minute."

"I didn't realize that was a two-man job," I teased.

"And they complain when we go to the ladies room together," Niqi chimed in. We all chuckled again.

"I hate to break this up, but I need to get back to making my rounds. It was very nice meeting you, Monique. Help yourself to whatever you want and I'll talk to you both later." Erica shook Niqi's hand again, kissed me on the cheek and brilliantly sashayed over to her other guests.

Half an hour and about thirty Sushi Rolls later, the Karma Notes lured almost everyone in the room onto the dance floor when they started playing Lionel Richie's, *All Night Long*. The guests flocked in droves; young, old and in between. Everybody was 'cutting up the rug', including Niqi and me.

The floor was crowded. Old folks were doing the hustle and the jitterbug, old-schoolers grooving to the Roger Rabbit, while Niqi and I were giving them the new-age "booty-hop." It was so much fun. We really could have danced all night long.

"Can I cut in?" I heard a man's voice say. I turned around to face Eric looking as charming as ever. Just looking at him made me giddy all over. He was so fine and dapper in his brand new Kenneth Cole suit.

"She's all yours," Monique responded. "I'll see y'all later. I see something I like, and I'm going to get it. Bye!" She shimmied her way over to the other side of the room.

About an hour later, Eric and I were all danced out. We made our way outside to get some cool air under the stars. A full moon was out and its reflection danced marvelously on the water. There were a few other couples lingering on the grounds, but we managed to find a corner that was a little more secluded.

"You are the most beautiful woman in that place. You know that, right?" He flattered me.

I blushed. He always made me blush. Trying to suppress my big, broadening smile, I shoved him gently on his shoulder.

"Oh stop, you must tell all the girls that. And besides, your sister looks amazing tonight," I replied.

"No, I only tell you that. And I'm not looking at my sister. I only got eyes for you, baby."

"Oh, Eric, you are so sweet. I have the best man in the world. I love you." I gushed all over him.

As our lips were about to meet, Erica came stomping around the corner toward us. She didn't look happy.

"What's wrong, Sis!" Eric jumped up in automatic defense of his twin.

"Sabrina, you really need to go check your girl," she advised.

"Who, Monique? What's wrong with her? Is she hurt?" Alarmed by her behavior, I started to head back into the party.

"Huh, not yet. But she's about to be, if you don't go in there and get her out of here." It was a little amusing to see her transform from the prissy princess to ghetto-fabulous.

"What the hell happened? Just calm down and tell me what happened." I stopped moving and waited for an answer, totally oblivious to what had taken place.

"She is all over Tony, and Karen is beside herself. Apparently Monique and Tony were dancing and shortly afterwards they were nowhere to be found. Karen later found them lip-locking in the garden. You know this whole separation thing is still fresh to Karen. I don't want this type of drama at my party, Sabrina. I didn't bargain for this. Please go and get your girl."

"Oh, my God. I'm sorry, Erica. Monique doesn't know anything about Tony and Karen. I'll go and talk to her and everything will be fine. Okay? So please, go back inside to Cameron and your guests and I'll take care of Monique. I'm sorry. Please don't let this ruin your night."

As I made my way toward the building, I felt Eric hold onto my arm.

"I'll come with you," he offered.

"No, stay with your sister. Calm her down and let me handle this. I'll be right back." I answered softly enough that Erica wouldn't hear me. I pecked him quickly on the mouth and left in search of Monique.

Karen was Erica and Eric's cousin. She was only two months estranged from an eight-year marriage. Everyone in the family was hopeful of an amicable reconciliation between her and Tony, and this little glitch involving my friend was not helping.

I looked everywhere for Monique and Tony: the dance floor, the balcony, the bathroom, the lobby. I searched in front, around, and behind the Country Club. They were nowhere to be found. I was so annoyed and frustrated, partly because my feet were killing me in these heels and mainly because I was embarrassed that *my* friend was ruining this party. By now everyone had been alerted as to what was going on.

After about forty-five minutes and two inflamed corns later, I finally caught a glimpse of two people walking toward the building from the parking lot. When they came close enough for me to identify them, I started limping toward their direction.

"Hey, Sabrina!" Niqi sang as soon as she saw me.

"Where were you?" I asked, sounding more like her mother, than her friend.

"I went to get something out of my car. Why are you looking at me like that?"

Without taking my eyes off Niqi, I firmly said, "Can you excuse us for a moment, Tony?" It was more of a command rather than a request.

"Um, yeah sure. Is everything all right?" Tony pestered.

This guy really didn't have a clue. "Everything's fine. I need to talk to my friend, thank you."

"It's okay, I'll see you later. Just give us a minute," Niqi assured him.

He rubbed her tenderly on the back and walked away.

"What are you doing?" I strained to get the question out. I was so angry. I know that Niqi usually never wasted any time when it came to men, but this was ridiculous.

"What the hell is your problem, Sabrina? Why are you acting like I stole your man?"

"Look, I realize that no one said anything to you, but you should know that Tony is married and his wife is not only here, she is also Eric and Erica's cousin."

"First of all, he's just about divorced and secondly, Erica said I could help myself to anything I wanted, and I did. So back off!"

"Did you sleep with him?" The moment the question escaped from my mouth, I knew it was a mistake.

The look on her face showed that she did not take kindly to it either. She was getting angry and I realized I needed to back down. I just didn't want any drama on Erica's special night, especially from someone who had accompanied *me*. It just didn't look good.

"You know what, I'm not even going to dignify that with an answer, Sabrina. And I don't appreciate you giving me the third degree. I danced with the man, we struck up a conversation and we clicked. We went for a walk and I had to get something out of my car. Now here we are, end of story!"

She obviously didn't realize that his wife had seen her and Tony making out in the dark. I decided not to say anything about it, because I really didn't like fighting with her like this.

"Okay, I'm sorry. I don't mean to be nasty, Niqi. It's just that those people in there are all family and they want Karen and her husband to work out their issues. You and Tony, with your fooling around, have taken the attention off Erica and Cameron, and placed it on Sabrina and her home-wrecking friend."

I tried my best to explain, but the more I said, the worse it sounded. This was supposed to be a night of celebration, not controversy. She raised her hands to her chest to illustrate that she was highly offended.

"Oh, so now I'm a home-wrecker..."

"That's not what I meant and you know it."

"No, what you meant was that I am an embarrassment to you and you don't want your high-class, sadiddy friends to believe that you could associate with someone like me. Well, that's just fine. I'll leave now, so that you don't have to feel *uncomfortable* around these pretentious people. This whole scene is way overdone and tacky anyway. I'm out."

Niqi turned her back to me and walked right back to her car. I almost tried to stop her, but decided not to. It was better that she left now, and we'd just talk about it tomorrow when things got calmer. We had had disagreements before and when we both calmed down, we would discuss it and that would be the end of it.

The remainder of the evening recommenced rather smoothly and Erica went back to being the happy bride-to-be she had been earlier. She and Cameron danced the night away while Eric and I went back to cuddling under the stars. At one point I saw Tony huddled romantically in a corner with Karen. They were talking, and that's all that mattered to anyone. For the moment, all seemed well with the world. I hoped it was all well with Niqi also.

From that day on, my friend was taboo around the Morrison camp, and needless to say, she was not invited to the wedding. But the worst of it was that she and Tony continued to see each other for months. The more I pleaded with her to leave him alone, the more defiant she became.

"We're in love!" she would profess.

"Yeah, but he's *married!*" I would mockingly remind her.

Five months into their affair, Niqi discovered that she was pregnant with his baby. She was very excited about it at first, but when she told him, the scumbag told her that he and his wife decided to work it out. He rationalized that it was really bad timing, and that having an illegitimate child would not be good for either of them.

A week later she remedied the situation by terminating the relationship and the pregnancy. It was her sixth abortion to date.

I never told Erica about it since Monique had already turned her off from the first day they met. She obviously discerned something in her that I couldn't, and now I wish I had heeded her warnings about my so-called friend. As soon as she came home I would tell her how right she was all along.

✦ ✦ ✦ ✦ ✦

The cold brick step I was sitting on had now become one with my rear end. Each cheek was almost frozen solid and was about two minutes away from being frostbitten. I stared wistfully into the streets, desperately hoping that every black Altima that passed was Erica's.

The urge to open and search the file was tempting, but it was soon repressed by the icy wind-chill factor that overpowered me. My fingers were cold enough in gloves. I couldn't bear subjecting them to the frigid air anymore.

My cell phone rang a few times, revealing Niqi as the caller, but I rejected them all and turned the ringer to vibrate. I wished Erica would hurry and come home so she could tell me what to do.

The time was going by. I noticed a few school buses making the rounds to unload students at their doorsteps. It was an indication that three o'clock had come and gone, and Erica had still not come home. As I stood to leave, I heard someone call out my name from above. I backed up from the steps and looked up. There was Erica, looking out the window with rows of pink curlers in her hair. Disappointment flooded my spirit.

"Please, don't tell me you've been here all this time," I whined.

"How long have you been sitting there?"

"A long time, Erica. I rang the doorbell three times. I really need to talk to you and it's freezing out here."

"I'm so sorry. There's Camille's bus. Okay, I'm coming down."

Within two minutes she was downstairs, wearing a navy blue terry-cloth robe and velvet slippers.

"I'm so sorry, Sabrina. My school was closed today. The doorbell broke a few days ago and Cameron hasn't had a chance to fix it yet. He left this morning for Arkansas on business. He'll be home tomorrow," she explained, after a warm embrace. "What's wrong? You look terrible." Erica noticed my cheerless disposition as soon as we let go of each other.

"We'll talk upstairs." I replied mysteriously.

I greedily scurried past her into the hallway to warm up. We waited behind closed doors until the noisy school bus came to a halt in front of the house. Once the driver pulled the lever that controlled the doors, the sweetest little girl emerged. Camille wore a navy blue-and-white plaid school uniform, white tights and black shoes, and carried a pink Dora the Explorer lunchbox. She came running up the steps, through the front door, and straight into her mother's arms, as fast as her little feet would allow.

"Hi, Auntie Sabrina," she cheered once she released her mother and ran to me for a hug and kiss.

"Hi, pretty girl. How was school today?" I did all I could to hide my despondency from her.

"Fine. Today was show-and-tell day. I brought my microphone and did a song for my class." Camille bragged about her performance as we ascended the tall, mahogany spiral staircase.

"Oh yeah, that's cool. What song did you sing?"

"*Hit Me Baby One More Time.* You wanna hear it?" she offered as we walked into the kitchen.

Erica immediately interjected. "Not right now, sweetie. Mommy and Auntie have to talk, so let's get you changed out of these school clothes, and then you can go into the den to watch Clifford. Okay?"

"Yes, Mommy."

"I would love to hear you sing it for me later. Would that be okay?" I asked.

"Okay, Auntie Sabrina," she replied gleefully.

"I'll be right back, Bri. I've got some Cheesecake left over from last night. It's in the fridge; help yourself. Just give me a few minutes." Erica pleaded before exiting the kitchen with a small bowl of sliced apples and a boxed juice in hand.

"Sure. I've been waiting this long. What's ten minutes more?" I teased.

The cheesecake sounded good. It was my favorite dessert, but I really didn't want anything to eat. I was way too anxious and just wanted to tell Erica about my discovery. I slid onto a bar stool at the granite countertop island in the center of the kitchen and waited for her to return.

Erica and Cameron truly had a splendid home; it was better than most of the homes I had seen on those reality shows where celebrities brag about their mansions. A posh living room furnished with all things Pier 1 and Ethan Allen, and an elegant formal dining room to comfortably fit twelve guests. The large eat-in kitchen was a chef's dream, decked out in granite, solid oak cabinets, and Viking stainless steel appliances. It was Cameron who did most of the cooking. The den was designed like the average living room, with plenty of room for Camille to play, being that she was not allowed to romp in the living room. The house had a total of six bedrooms, three full and two half bathrooms, and an extra oversized media room on the lower level of the house, strictly designed for entertaining on game or movie nights.

The entertainment room was my favorite place in the house because it boasted a large pool table, wooden wet-bar, stone fireplace, a Bose home theater system with surround sound, a 52-inch flat screen television, computer, DVD and VCR player, Xbox, Play Station and a library of CDs and movies. It had plush carpeting, a huge leather sectional and a pull-out couch, just in case they accommodated overnight guests.

This place was especially fun on game nights, which happened at least twice a month. Erica would serve the food and I would run the bar, and tips were expected for the impeccable service. Eric and I loved hanging out here, and always swore that we, too, would own a brownstone home someday.

"That little girl is a piece of work," Erica joked playfully about her daughter as she returned to the kitchen.

"She's getting so big. And what does she know about *Hit Me Baby One More Time!*" I exclaimed about Camille.

"I know. Britney Spears has invaded the soul of my three-year-old. But she's so cute though."

"She really is, Erica."

"Now tell me, what could possibly be so bad that it would have you sitting outside of my house, waiting in the freezing cold for me to come home on my day off?"

She pulled up a stool and sat across from me. I didn't even know where to start, so I pulled out the folder and put it on the table. She glanced at it, and then looked up curiously at me.

"Eric's cheating on me!" I just blurted it out. There was just no better way to say it. I opened the file, removed all of the pictures and handed them to her. "He's having an affair with Monique, Erica. You were right about her all along, and now I wish I had listened to you. What am I going to do?" A fresh well of tears sprang forth.

"Oh, Jesus! Sabrina... Damn it, Eric... Oh, my God!" Erica jumbled her thoughts as she flicked through the disgraceful photographs.

When she was done, she put them down and looked at me with tears in her eyes. "I'm so sorry, Bri. I'm so sorry you had to find out like this." She paused to gather her thoughts, and then continued. "Sabrina, I have a confession to make."

Now, I was the curious one. I cocked my head to the side and then nodded for her to continue. She got up from the stool and walked over to the cabinet and removed two wineglasses. Then she removed a bottle of Merlot from the wine rack and poured a generous amount into each glass. She gave one to me and guzzled hers in three seconds. Erica then returned to her stool. She was making me so nervous. I couldn't even touch my drink.

"About a month and a half ago, Cameron, Camille and I went away to Orlando to use our week at the timeshare. Do you remember that?"

"Yeah. You guys took Camille to Disney and she got food poisoning from some Chinese restaurant. I remember." I was anxious for her to get to the point.

"Good. Well, we came back two days earlier than expected and promised Camille that she could watch TV in her room until she felt better. When we got home, I went down to the game room to get a few videos for her.

When I turned on the light, I saw Eric and that little slut going at it on top of the bar counter. They didn't even hear me come in. I was so shocked that I just started screaming.

They snapped out of it and scrambled for something to cover up. Eric tried to offer some sort of weak explanation, but I was so furious that I just told him to 'shut the ...' Well, you know. I told Monique to get out of my house, and told her if *ever* I saw her near my property again, I would shoot her. She put on most of her clothes and ran out of here really fast. Sabrina ..."

I started to bawl. "Oh, my God, Erica! A month and a half ago? You knew about this all along and you didn't tell me? I thought you were my friend!"

"I wanted to, Sabrina. I threatened Eric that I would tell you, but he swore that he would fix it, and made me promise to keep his secret. He's my brother... I didn't know what to do. When I talked to Cameron about it, he advised me not to get involved. I'm sorry; please don't be angry with me."

She struggled to find the right explanation, but there was none.

"You knew! Every time I came over here, you knew. God, I must've looked like such a fool. You helped them make a fool out of me, Erica. I know he's your brother, but I thought you were my friend. I was obviously wrong." I gathered my belongings, dried my tears and made my way to the stairs.

She scuttled behind me, tears flooding her face. "He still loves you, you know. He wants to work it out; he's just caught up. Sabrina, please, say something."

"Good bye, Erica." I said. And closed the door behind me.

Chapter 5

It was only four o'clock in the afternoon and my apartment was in complete darkness. Every blind was closed shut and all the curtains were drawn to keep out the sunlight. This was one of the gripes I had about having a roommate.

Claudia Hernandez was a quiet and rather peculiar Colombian woman, and she laid claim to the title 'born-again Christian'. We had been sharing the apartment for almost two years now, and she had these bizarre tendencies that irritated me. I had to admit that she was the best roommate, out of a line of four priors, all of whom didn't last six months. She paid her rent on time, she was neat, clean, and most of all she stayed out of my way. We didn't have a bad relationship. In fact, it was rather decent. I guess me being away at Eric's for weeks at a time didn't hurt and whenever I was home we chatted about insignificant matters like the weather, and our jobs.

I really tried to avoid getting into deep conversations with Claudia, especially because I did not want her to try and convert me to her religion as so many other Christian people had tried before. I appreciated her consideration and respect for my feelings, although, at times she would subtly leave "God" stuff around the apartment.

I once confronted her about her habit of drawing the curtains so tight, and she explained that it was only when she prayed. She said she needed her space to be "still and quiet, blocking out all distractions" whenever she went into the presence of God. I asked her if she could let that space be in the privacy of her own room, that way no one would be inconvenienced.

Claudia may have been offended, but she never complained, and to be perfectly honest, I could not have cared less.

It had been at least a week and a half since I had last been here, so she probably decided to live a little. When the cat is away, the mice will play. Well, the cat is back and here to stay, so whatever liberties she was used to were about to come to an abrupt end.

I opened all the drapes, allowing the sun to illuminate the room, and cracked the window a bit for some fresh air. Although it was cold outside, the apartment was hot and muggy. It seemed as though Claudia, too had not been here for a few days, because unopened mail addressed to her lay among the pile under the mail slot. I separated the mail and left hers on the kitchen table. She had left a note on the fridge saying she had an emergency and would be out of town for a week.

There wasn't much food to choose from in the refrigerator and even though I had eaten both bags of peanuts, I was still very hungry. I found a can of tuna, and there was bread and mayonnaise, so I settled for a tuna fish sandwich. I brought the food, my mail, the folder and my purse with me to my bedroom.

The scene in my room immediately deflated me. There was "Eric and Sabrina" memorabilia all over the place. Pictures of us were everywhere on the walls, dresser and nightstand. Souvenirs from the many vacation spots we toured and a mountain of jewelry was strewn about on the dresser. Half of the clothes in my wardrobe had also been gifts from Eric, expressing his everlasting commitment to me.

Bridal magazines, catalogs, and wedding-planning books were spread out all over the computer desk. Several teddy bears and other stuffed animals lined the shelves on the walls, and a few of my favorites sat in a neat row against the pillows on my bed. All were courtesy of Eric Morrison.

I dropped the things I carried onto the nightstand and in one swoop, cleared all the stuffed animals off the pillow onto the floor. Without barely any energy left, I collapsed my heavily laden body onto my inviting bed. I reached to the floor for the biggest bear and held it close to me.

What was I going to do? I had not the faintest idea how to handle something like this. I am supposed to be married in eight months and my fiancé is having an affair with my best friend. It sounded like a topic for the Jerry Springer Show.

As reluctant as I felt about researching the contents of Monique's file, I was determined to know the truth. It would be better for me to make a decision with all the facts laid out than to be in denial about the whole thing. I sat on the edge of the bed and cupped my hands over my face. I needed just a few minutes to pull my mind together.

No longer craving food, I placed the plate with the sandwich on the floor and reached for my purse and the folder on the nightstand. The vibrations from my cell phone pulsated through my bag. When I checked, there were now sixteen missed calls displayed on the screen. Three were from Eric and the remaining thirteen from Niqi. It crossed my mind to return Eric's calls, but that thought faded quickly, as soon as I glanced at the folder. I put the phone down and braced myself.

3/9

Dear Eric,

I wanted to apologize for my behavior yesterday evening after we dropped Sabrina at the airport. It was way out of line and very disrespectful. I love Sabrina and would never do anything to intentionally hurt her, but I don't know what came over me. Truthfully speaking, I always dreamed of what kissing

you would be like and I acted before I thought. Once again, I'm sorry and I don't blame you for not speaking to me ever again.
Sincerely Yours,
M. H.

March... March. Where did I go in March? I tried to recall and then it came back to me.

My grandmother fell ill when her nurse was away on vacation. Grandie wasn't comfortable with the replacement aide her insurance company had sent her, so I went to Georgia to care for her. I wasn't sure how long I would be gone and Niqi insisted on accompanying Eric and me to the airport. I was only gone for a little more than a month, and never once did it cross my mind that this conniving back-stabber would make a move on my man.

Did she plan this? I wondered if this was a calculated attempt to manipulate the circumstances surrounding my family crisis. I had found it a little strange when she persistently nagged me for my expected date of return. But Niqi was like that, relentless about everything. I never gave it a second thought after that.

3/19
Dearest Eric,

I was so happy you called. Thank you for accepting my apology, and no, you don't have to worry about me blabbing to Bri. I couldn't hurt her like that. She is under so much stress over her grandma's stroke. I miss her a lot, but I must say that it was really great talking to you for so long. Did you realize we spoke on the phone for like three hours? I almost didn't make it to work the next day. (Smile)

    I won't pretend Eric, it was truly worth it; you were worth it. As I promised, I still want to make you that full course meal to make it up to you. If you're not busy this weekend, I would be honored if you would join me on Saturday evening for dinner, my place. I'll call you to confirm on Thursday.

Yours,
Niqi H.

I seriously thought I would explode at any moment. Fury stirred in me as I read Niqi's own account of the scheme she devised to set Eric up. I know how she thinks. Niqi knew exactly what she was doing. And Eric... what a fool he was to have fallen for her deliberate scheme. Didn't he see it coming? I wondered if he even cared. He of all people knew how Niqi was, and yet he still managed to walk right into her snare; totally disregarding the effect it would have on me and our relationship.

    Why Eric?

3/25

    Oh, my God, Eric! What did we do? I noticed you haven't called me since you left my house on Saturday and I understand. I'm sooo sorry! How can we fix this? I'm okay with pretending it never happened, if that's what you want. I feel so horrible about this. I don't know what else to say but *please return my calls or e-mail me so we can make this right. For what it's worth though Eric, I personally enjoyed every minute of it. Please call me.*

Niqi.

I was all cried out by the time I read the third letter and my chest felt like it was about to cave in. My imagination cruelly betrayed me as I unwittingly visualized them engaging in their debauchery. I couldn't read anymore. I was exhausted, angry and depressed. I wearily transferred everything to the floor, curled up in the fetal position and before I knew it, I was asleep.

The clap of lightning and thunder frightened me out of my well-needed rest. I awoke feeling dazed and groggy. It was dark outside and the fluorescent red digits on the clock radio read 7:23 p.m. I stayed in bed for a few seconds, trying to get my mind to focus. Then I quickly realized that it was not raining outside and the continuous clamor was the sound of raucous banging on my front door.

I got up and stealthily walked out of my room into the hallway. Making my way to the door, I carefully tried to minimize the creaking of the floorboards with every step. The pounding continued. Desperately trying not to make a sound, I placed my eye over the peephole to see who the imbecile was.

"Sabrina, open the door! I know you are standing there, because you just blocked the street light shining in the kitchen window."

Damn!

"Open the damn door, Sabrina. What the hell is wrong with you? Why did you stand me up today? You could have called me."

I opened the door. Monique actually looked bewildered. I didn't know how I was going to handle her, but I wanted to get it over and done with.

"What is going on with you today? If you wanted to cancel, you should have just called me. I had other things to do, you know."

She stepped into my house, a whiff of *Curve*, Eric's signature cologne, trailing behind her.

"Yeah, I bet. Like Eric?"

"Excuse me?"

"Why don't *you* tell *me* what's going on, Niqi?" I demanded.

She rapidly turned around, her long weave swinging with her. "What do you mean, Sabrina? What is this?"

"How dare you come into my house playing dumb and acting like I'm stupid? I know, Niqi!" I began to scream at her. "I know, you little whore, okay! I know that you're sleeping with Eric."

I could tell by the expression on her face that she wasn't expecting that. She looked like someone had just kicked her in the teeth.

I stood there looking and waiting for her to respond. She staggered a bit and made her way to the couch where she just plopped down. Then came the waterworks.

"Oh, my God, Sabrina. I'm so sorry. I..."

I had to cut her off. "Sorry, Niqi? That's all you've got to say to me? SORRY! You ruin the most important thing to me, and all you can say is that you're 'sorry'? Get the *hell* out of my house. Get out!"

"Bri, wait. I swear, I never meant for this to happen. It just happened. You of all people should know that I never meant to hurt you. I violated our friendship and I broke your trust, and I am so sorry."

I lowered my voice and spoke tersely. "You're not sorry, Niqi, not for what you did. You're sorry that you got caught. If you were sorry, it would have ended after the first, or second, or even the third time you were screwing *my* man. He's the one thing that means the world to me, and you had to destroy it. You are an evil witch, you know that, right? Everybody tried to warn me about you, but no-o-o, I wanted to show them that there was goodness and decency in Monique Henry. So what, she had like SIX abortions! Everybody makes mistakes. She's not a product of her environment, just an ordinary girl trying to make something good out of the obstacles in her life.

"But that's not the truth though, is it, Niqi? No, you are exactly the slut everyone says you are. You're a taker and a thief, and you sabotage *everything* that is good, just to get what you want. To hell with everybody else, right, Niqi?"

She sat there staring blankly at me and didn't utter a word. I wanted to dice her with my tongue, the way she had sliced my heart into a million pieces. My voice dropped to a whisper, and I continued.

"So, how long have you been watching and waiting, and planning to make your move, Niqi? Hmm, the night at Klub Elektric? The week before I left for Georgia? When, Niqi?"

Still, she gave no answer.

"You're so pathetic that you can't even see that you are just an object to him. And to every other man who comes in and out of your life, for that matter."

I looked her up and down, shaking my head pitifully at her, until finally she spoke.

"I understand that you're hurt and that we are to blame, and I really am sorry. I didn't plan this Sabrina, I swear on my mother's grave. It just happened. I never..."

"*It just happened!*" I interjected loudly. "Spit happens, Niqi. You screwing my man for months on end, that sweetie, is cold, calculated betrayal. Never mind though, your days of playing Eric's whore are over. He loves *me*; he's going to marry *me*, and there's nothing you can do to change that."

I started to laugh mockingly in her face. Monique got up from the sofa and tore into me.

"You can say what you want to, Sabrina. But since we are being so honest I should let you know that Eric loves me too, and I love him."

"*Loves you!*" I laughed harder and louder this time, and could feel every vein in my face begin to pulsate. She had gone mad.

"Look at you, scrounging after my husband. Eric doesn't love you anymore than a Jew loves swine, Monique. You are really crazy if you think that. Toya must've sewn that weave in way too tight this time."

"Whatever, Sabrina. He's not your husband yet; and besides, I saw him first."

"That you did. But he chose *me*, and it's killing you. It killed you then, and it's been killing you for the past five years. Well just in case you forgot, I'm the one with the ring, Niqi," I said, flaunting my rock in her face. "The only ring I see you with is the one around your collar. Get out of my house, now!"

She picked up her bag from the couch and made her way to the door. With one hand on the knob, she turned to me and said, "Again, I really am sorry that I hurt you, and that things had to turn out this way, Bri. But I regret even more to tell you that I'm three months pregnant, and I'm keeping *this* one. And yes, Eric is the daddy." She turned to open the door.

"You lying heifer!" I screamed at her, and before she could get out, I lunged toward her, grabbing onto her Yaki mane, dragging her back into the apartment. We fought and wrestled till we wound up on the floor. Rage consumed me and I wanted to kill her!

"Get off of me, Sabrina! You are going to hurt my baby!" Monique pleaded.

"Good, I'll kill the both of you!" I screamed, desperately wanting to stomp on Monique's belly.

"Sabrina! What are you doing?" I felt someone hurl me off Monique. Completely surprised, I turned to see Claudia and another woman who resembled her, standing in my living room.

Claudia lifted Monique up to her feet and asked, "Are you okay?"

"If something has happened to my child, I swear you'll pay for this, Sabrina." Monique cried, as she ran out of the apartment, looking disheveled and spent.

"You New Yorkers really know how to get down. Claudia, now I'm glad that I came with you," said the woman with a heavy Spanish accent, standing next to Claudia. She then made her way to the sofa; intently watching us like this was an episode of *Days of Our Lives*.

"Calla te Silvia, por favor," Claudia hushed her, and turned to me with a genuine look of dismay on her face. "What is the meaning of this, Sabrina? What is the matter?"

I was panting and crying so hard that I just fell to my knees. Claudia fell to the floor right along with me and held me as I wailed on her shoulders. I cried and cried until I was motionless and let the tears just flow. It hurt so bad. I had lost so much in this one day and I didn't know how I was going to go on. I wasn't sure I wanted to; what for? Life never ceased to sucker-punch me right where it hurt. Everything I hold dear always gets taken from me.

Oh God, why me?

"Shhh, it's okay. Whatever it is Sabrina, we'll get through it, I promise honey. Weeping may endure for a night, but joy comes in the morning." Claudia rocked me in her arms and I felt so safe. Her words were so soothing and before I realized it, I had stopped crying.

"You want to talk about it?" she inquired.

I wanted to, but I just didn't have the strength to talk.

"Mm mm," I moaned, shaking my head.

"Okay, sweetie. Let's get you into bed. C'mon," she continued, as she helped me to my feet and walked me to my room. Feeling a tad bit better, I managed to sit up in the bed.

"Would you like me to make you some tea, Sabrina?" Claudia offered.

I looked up to her and said, "She's pregnant, Claudia. She's going to have Eric's baby."

As if she hadn't heard my shocking news, Claudia stuck her head out the door and said, "Silvia, please make a cup of chamomile tea for Sabrina. It's in the cupboard above the microwave." She left the door ajar, and then sat next to me on the bed. Claudia took my hand in hers and spoke softly.

"Believe it or not, but I know this story all too well, Sabrina. I know that gut-wrenching anguish you are feeling right now and all I can say is that this too shall pass. My ex-husband had an ongoing affair with my only sister, and eventually left me to be with her. I never thought I would get through it, let alone past it, but the Lord became the source of my strength and He healed my shattered heart, and gave me such peace that I could never describe it in words. And you know what? He can do the same for you. I will not lie and tell you that it happens overnight, but it will happen."

Silvia tapped lightly on the door and Claudia got up and took the hot cup from her.

"Now, I want you to drink this tea and go to your bed. It will help to settle you. I'll be here in the morning. Okay, sweetie?"

I nodded. "Thanks, Claudia." I said meekly.

She smiled and turned to leave, closing the door behind her. I changed into my PJs, drank my tea and sought a peaceful end to this long and dreary day.

Chapter 6

I woke up around four o'clock in the morning, drenched in urine. I could not believe that had I peed my bed. Still half asleep, I leaped out of bed and staggered to the bathroom. As soon as I turned on the light, it became apparent that I was bleeding. My entire pajama bottoms were soaked in blood. I dropped to the bathroom floor in panic and screamed out for Claudia. Within a minute she ran in and saw what was going on. As fast as she came in, she darted back out, and I could hear her on the phone giving the 9-1-1 dispatchers the address to our apartment.

"Hold on, Sabrina, the ambulance will be here soon."

Claudia brought me some towels and wrapped my bottom half so that the blood could be absorbed and not continue to seep onto the bathroom mats. Even though I was embarrassed to have her see me in yet another undignified state, she managed to keep me calm and together as I sat in the pool of blood. I barely knew her and whenever we had interacted, it was usually so superficial, at least on my part. In spite of that, she was still compassionate and seemed genuinely concerned about my dilemma.

"Are you in pain, honey?" she inquired.

I shook my head. I had no idea what the problem was but I was feeling no pain. There was just an intense tightening in my stomach, which I assumed was probably gas-related. I had hardly eaten anything the day before.

The EMT people were in my apartment within twenty minutes and by that time Claudia had already changed into jeans and a sweater.

"You don't have to come with me," I explained. "I'll be fine. Stay with your guest."

"Nonsense! I'm coming with you. My sister will be fine, I left her a note as to where we will be and she has my cell number."

Claudia was too good to be true. Where did she come from, and was that the same sister she told me about last night? It couldn't be. I nodded and we left in the ambulance together.

The nurses on staff in the emergency room rushed me to a private room marked OB/GYN. By the time we got there, the bleeding had already stopped, and one of the nurses took my blood pressure and requested a urine sample. Claudia was instructed to stay behind in the waiting room to fill out the paperwork, but I insisted that she remain with me. Initially, they refused, but they soon relented when they realized that I would not take "no" for an answer.

The room they put me in was cold, and after Claudia filled out as much of my information as she could, she went to ask for an extra blanket for me. Not only was the heat not on high enough in this place, but the extremely thin hospital gowns they make you wear practically exposed all my assets. I seriously needed a pair of underwear. By the time Claudia returned, the doctor had just entered the room.

"Good morning, Miss Richards. My name is Dr. Patricia Valentine, but you can call me Dr. Val."

She was a petite, young black woman, who could not have been more than thirty-five years old. She was impressive and confident in her stance and I immediately felt comfortable with her as my physician. She stood next to my bed with her clipboard and pen in hand.

"Hi, Dr. Val. Do you know what's wrong with me?" I inquired, a hint of fear in my voice.

"Well, I'd like to ask you a few questions first. Are you in any pain?"

"No, not really. Just a little tightening in my stomach, but I barely had anything to eat all day yesterday, so it could be gas," I answered.

"Is there any possibility that you are pregnant?"

"Huh," I snickered. "No, I'm on the Depo-Provera shot."

The doctor speedily wrote down my responses and continued with her questions.

"When was your last period and when are you scheduled for your next shot?"

"Um, about five months ago, and I have an appointment next week."

"Have you been experiencing any spotting or unusual discharge?"

"Ah, not really. Why, what seems to be the problem?"

She continued. "Miss Richards, the lab results from your urine sample came back with high levels of HCG and to confirm whether or not you are in fact pregnant, I'd like to perform an ultrasound."

"Why? I just told you, I'm on birth control."

"I know. However, it is not uncommon for a woman to become pregnant while taking birth control and no birth control is one hundred percent effective, especially if not applied correctly or in a timely manner," Dr. Val educated me.

"You seem to be hemorrhaging to some extent and although the bleeding has stopped we want to rule out an ectopic pregnancy or miscarriage as the source of your bleeding."

She had to be crazy. There was no way I was pregnant and certainly not at a time like this when my whole life was in crisis. She could do a hundred ultrasounds if she wanted to. Pregnancy was just not possible. No way, no how.

"Okay, yeah. Sure, I'll do it," I conceded.

Dr. Val left the room and fifteen minutes later she was back with the ultrasound machine. Claudia was quiet for most of the time, but her presence alone was comforting and helped to put me at ease. As the doctor began to ooze that awfully cold gel on my belly, Claudia moved closer to the bed to hold my hand.

A small part of me wanted to laugh, because if someone were to walk in the room it would appear that Claudia and I were expecting a child together. Then again, maybe it's not that funny because a scenario like that is quite prevalent in today's world.

"Can you see that," said Dr. Val, pointing to the monitor of the machine, as she moved that wand-like instrument all over my abdomen.

"I see a whole lot of nothing, Dr. Val." All I could make out was mass blurriness and a couple of circles.

"You see this?" she asked, pointing to one of the circles. "That, Miss Richards, is a fetus. And this," she continued, pointing at the other circle, "is another fetus. You are pregnant with twins," she concluded, very matter-of-factly.

I sat there stunned, eyes bulging and mouth open, staring intently at the hazy screen. What was she talking about, pregnant? And two? I didn't see what she saw. Those were circles, not babies.

God, this couldn't possibly get any worse.

She turned off the machine, cleaned off my belly and asked Claudia to excuse us.

"Are you all right, sweetie?" Claudia asked me. All I could do was nod.

"All right, I'll be right outside," she said, and left me alone with Doctor "Bad News Brown".

Dr. Val detached the printed information from the machine and then moved it to the other side of the room. She pulled up a stool next to my bed and sat down.

"According to the ultrasound, I have confirmed that you are indeed pregnant, and that you are probably bordering on eight weeks. Bleeding in the first trimester is not very unusual. It is usually painless and stops by itself if you stay off your feet and avoid intercourse or any strenuous activities. You indicated that you felt slight cramping, and for this reason, I want to monitor you for the remainder of the morning and throughout the day. Bleeding with cramping is more alarming and is usually a sign of a miscarriage in the making. Unfortunately, there is no way to stop a pregnancy loss at this time, so we usually recommend that you watch and wait in these situations. Do you have any questions so far, Miss Richards?"

My mind was going a mile a minute and I was overwhelmed. I was not ready to have any children and especially not now, when chaos was rampant in every path of my life. I had no job, no family, no friends, and now, no fiancé. What was I going to do with two babies?

Yes, I had a ton of questions, yet nothing came out of my mouth. I just stared blankly at her and shook my head. She moved in a little closer, put her clipboard on the table and continued talking.

"When a pregnant woman is subjected to violence, it is certainly a threat to her own health, but it also puts the fetus at risk. Now, everything we talk about is kept strictly confidential. I noticed a couple of bruises on your arm, coupled with the bleeding, so I have to ask if you are at risk for physical abuse."

Dr. Val was very perceptive. I didn't even realize any marks were left from the fight Monique and I had last night. There they were; two big black-and-blue marks on the upper part of my left arm.

"No, Dr. Val. I was in a bit of a scuffle yesterday, with a friend, or rather an ex-friend. My fiancé doesn't beat me."

I still referred to Eric as my fiancé. Anything else would have to take a little getting used to.

"Okay, I see. Miss Richards, I must tell you that that 'scuffle' almost resulted in you losing your pregnancy. I understand you were not aware of your condition, but it is imperative that you be extremely cautious from here on out. The good news is that your cervix was not ruptured and both heartbeats seem to be stable. We are not able to pinpoint the exact cause of bleeding, but you must take it easy. I want you to understand that stress-related factors and/or direct physical injuries may cause adverse effects in one or both of the unborn babies. If you don't have any other questions, I'll leave you to rest. I'll be back in a few hours to check on you. Would you like your friend to come back in?"

"No, thank you. I'm tired and I want to be alone. Could you tell her thanks for everything, and I'll call her later."

"All right, Miss Richards. If and when you are ready for something to eat or if you need anything, just press the red button behind you and the nurse on duty will respond. I'll see you in awhile. Try to get some rest."

"Thank you, Dr. Val," I said.

She smiled and left, closing the door behind her. I hoped Claudia wasn't upset. She had been so kind to me but I just didn't want to be around anybody right now. The apartment was only a ten dollar cab ride away and I would just have to pay her back.

The sun had already come up. Curious to know the time, I reached over to the chair to get my phone out of my purse. Stuck between the flip and the dial pad was the pamphlet I received from that irritating woman on the train yesterday.

NOW WHAT? GIVE JESUS THE CHANCE TO MAKE IT RIGHT.

That was the headline. I started to read it and halfway through, images of Eric making love to Monique began to flood my mind. Did he touch her the same way as he did me? Who did he enjoy more? I put the tract back in the purse. I couldn't concentrate on it.

It was twenty minutes to seven. I had eighteen more missed calls and urgent messages from Eric. I wanted so badly to call him and alert him as to what was going on, but I didn't have the energy it would take to deal with him. It wasn't long before my eyes got heavy and soon exhaustion overtook me, lulling me off to sleep. I was grateful.

Chapter 7

The smell of fried chicken, sweet potatoes and collard greens penetrated my subconscious and stirred me out of my sleep. Still in a daze, I immediately presumed Claudia had brought me something to eat. Heaven knows, I truly did not want to experiment with any of this hospital food. I turned over to see who else but Eric sitting in the chair next to my bed. On top of the windowsill was a beautiful bouquet of two dozen red roses and three *Get Well Soon* balloons.

I wondered if he thought that was all it would take to make me well anytime soon.

He looked terrible and stressed, as if he hadn't slept in weeks. His clothes were wrinkled and unkempt and knowing the well-put-together man that he is, I could tell Niqi had let the cat out of the bag.

There he sat, staring at me, looking like a little boy who just got caught with his hand in the cookie jar. He got up to kiss my forehead and I turned away briskly so that he would feel my repulsion. He picked up one of my hands and held it to his chest and, as much as I knew I should, I didn't pull away. I realized that I still loved him and in spite of everything I had discovered. I felt maybe there was a way we could work through it. I began to take into account the amount of time and energy that had been invested in our relationship. Besides, I wasn't going to let Monique have him without putting up a fight, so I was willing to hear what he had to say.

"What do you want, Eric?" I asked in a whisper.

"I came to see you, baby. I've been calling you since yesterday, all day and night, and when I stopped by your apartment this morning, your roommate's sister told me where you were. I came right away and the nurse told me you had just fallen asleep. I've been here since eight o' clock this morning. I brought you some food from Sweet Audrey's. I know the food here can't be good. Why are you in here? What happened? Are you all right?" He got up to put the food next to the flowers and stepped closer to the bed.

Silvia must have given him the note Claudia left for her. The food smelled great and if my appetite was in tact I would have certainly enjoyed every bite. Eric knew that Sweet Audrey's was my favorite restaurant in Harlem. But it would take much more than Audrey's soul food to cure my anguished soul.

"No, I'm not all right, Eric!" I snapped. "And seeing that it took you until this morning to get to my house, it's safe to assume that you were held up by Monique. I'm sure your honey briefed you about our little altercation."

"Damn, baby. Damn, damn, damn! I messed up baby, I messed up big time," he offered.

"Is that what you call it Eric? 'Messed up big time!' Sleeping with my best friend and getting her pregnant?"

I started to cry. I tried not to, but I couldn't help it.

"How could you do something like this to us, Eric? Do you have any idea how much I'm hurting right now? *Do you?* Did you forget we have plans to start a life together? If you had second thoughts about our engagement, you could have been honest with me. What happened? I just don't understand, Eric. You have to help me understand what went wrong."

My voice trembled at every word spoken.

"Baby, I'm so sorry that I've been lying to you. I don't know what happened. It just happened, and then it just got out of hand."

"No, Eric, it didn't 'just happen'. *You* allowed this to happen. You've been cheating on me with my best friend for eight whole months and then you knock her up. Eight freaking months, Eric! What did she do for you that I didn't, huh?"

"It's not like that, Bri. Damn."

In all the years I had known him, this is the first time his vocabulary was limited to the word "damn."

"What is it then, Eric? Tell me, please. I really need to know why I wasn't enough for you."

I bit my bottom lip so hard I tasted blood. I wouldn't cry in front of him anymore.

"It's not you, Sabrina. You're wonderful and perfect, and everything a man could hope for..."

"Just not good enough for you though, huh, Eric? What does Monique have, or better yet, what does she do for you that I don't? I dedicated my whole life to you. How could you sell us out for someone as cheap as Monique? You know what, never mind. I get it now. You want a whore, not a wife. I thought I knew you. How could I have been so wrong?"

I had a million questions and I wanted him to say something that would help me to understand. Instead, he just stood there with his head down, looking at the floor like an idiot.

"I realize that Erica knows about this, but what about your parents? Do they know you've been playing house with the likes of Monique Henry?" I asked, suddenly aware that they will also be affected by this indecent affair. He kept looking down and shook his head.

"Do you see how selfish you are, Eric? Mom and Dad have already paid for half of the cost of the wedding, and you go and do something like this? How could you do this to me? *To us?*"

He didn't answer.

"So what now, Eric? Where do we go from here?"

More silence. I could see the tears forming in his eyes and then falling to the bed. He put my hand down and rubbed his hands over his head.

"I don't know. I don't know what to do or say. I'm so sorry to put you through this, baby!"

"*Oh, my God.* Eric, do you actually *love* her? She told me that you love her. Is it true?" Shock and disbelief was written all over my face.

He still kept his head down. "Look at me, dammit!" I barked at him.

"I still love you," he answered.

"I didn't ask you that, Eric. Are you in love with Monique?"

He looked into my eyes and sighed deeply. "I don't know."

Grief and heartache viciously overcame me with such heaviness that I wanted to die. For a few moments, it seemed like time had stopped. The room felt like it was closing in on me and my entire being had gone numb. My soul ached from the sting of betrayal. There was nothing anyone could say or do to make it feel better. I loathed him right then and there. I hated him with a passion for sharing the affection reserved for me with another woman. I don't know what hurt more, the cheating factor, or the fact that Monique was the other woman. She was supposed to be my friend.

I decided not to say anything to him about the babies I was carrying in my womb. I really didn't see the point. I wanted to hurt him as much as he had hurt me, and it was at that moment that I realized what had to be done. My body shook as I bawled uncontrollably. He moved closer to put his arms around me in an effort to console me in my agony, but I did not want him near me.

"Don't flipping touch me!" I snarled. "Don't you ever touch me again, you bastard."

Eric backed up so fast; he didn't know what hit him. He had never seen me this way, and by the look on his face I could tell he was shocked. Just then, there was a quick knock on the door, and in walked a nurse with some paperwork in her hand.

"Excuse me, Miss Richards. I'm very sorry to disturb you, but your insurance information is missing on the forms that your friend filled out for you earlier, and we cannot process your claim without it."

I wiped my face and tried to regain my composure before taking the forms from her. She then quickly turned to leave.

The tension in the room was so thick that you probably *couldn't* cut it with a knife. Eric stood in silence. Looking over the papers, I suddenly remembered that Hilton had fired me the day before, so I had no health insurance. Before the nurse exited, I called out to her.

"Can you please bill this as self-pay, because as of yesterday I have no medical insurance?"

Her eyes widened, suggesting that this visit was going to be expensive.

"Do you have any idea how much it's going to cost?"

"Well, Miss Richards, I can't provide you with a specific cost, but we can work out a payment plan to fit your budget."

"I don't have a budget, nurse. I'm unemployed," I said, obviously annoyed.

Eric looked alarmed and interjected, "You lost your job, baby?"

I ignored him. Looking at the nurse, he continued, "Whatever it is, you can send the bill to me."

"I don't need your money, Eric! This is my damn business, and I don't need or want your help," I retorted forcefully.

The nurse looked at me with pleading eyes that begged for relief from the increasingly tense argument.

I reiterated my previous instruction and she gladly took back the forms, and practically dashed out of the room into the hallway.

"Sabrina, can we please talk about this? I know you are hurt, but I want us to deal with this. Please, baby."

Eric didn't even wait for the door to close before he started yapping again.

"You said everything I need to hear, Eric. I don't want to hear anything else from you. Please leave."

"Sabrina..."

"I'm serious, Eric. Get out. Go be with your baby's mother and leave me alone. I hope the two of you have a miserable life together." I turned over, giving my back to him and pulled the thin hospital sheet over my head.

"Oh, and you can take your worthless flowers with you too. I don't want that crap in here."

I wanted to hurt him, and I knew he was offended.

He walked to the door, opened it and retorted, "What about the ring? Do you still want that?"

That did it! I took off the ring and flung it at him so hard it ricocheted off his chest and rolled onto the floor. He could keep his stupid ring. It was useless to me now anyway. Niqi always liked it; maybe he'd give it to her. I was so angry that I began to shout ferociously, hurling expletives and profanities at him. The outburst created such a commotion that two male attendants rushed into the room.

Eric lowered his head in despair and walked out with the men, leaving me behind, to walk into the arms of another woman.

)⌒ •)⌒ •)⌒)⌒ •)⌒ •

Dr. Val discharged me late that afternoon. She concluded that the babies were stable and had a good chance of surviving. She also gave me firm orders to watch my stress level and provided instructions on how to take it easy. She even allotted me a few months supply of vitamin samples to bring home, which I thought was comical, especially since I had already decided to terminate the pregnancy. You could say that I learned a thing or two from Monique.

I know it was a selfish thing to do, but I wasn't going to be a common statistic and play the role of some man's 'baby-mother'. I had too many dreams and plans set for my life, and Eric's bastard babies were not going to ruin them. I also knew that the babies were not to blame, but I could see no way to make a good life for them. Part of my decision was out of concern for them. I had to look out for all our best interests.

No, this was the right thing to do. I chose not to tell Dr. Val about my decision. She had been so thorough and caring with me, I didn't want to disappoint her in her efforts in helping me. So, I just shook her hand and thanked her sincerely for everything.

Chapter 8

The cab driver overcharged me by five dollars for the ride to my apartment, but I was too exhausted to protest or complain. I was happy to be out of the hospital and looked forward to the comfort of my own bed. I needed to sit and think. I had been through hell in the past two days and I had to put things in perspective. But first, I decided to have a couple of shots of *After Shock* from the liquor cabinet in the living room. It always helped to calm me down and under the circumstances, it was the most appropriate drink for me now. I thought about the babies' health for a second but soon shrugged it off. Abortion was my final answer.

The television was on in the living room when I stepped into the apartment, but no one was there. On the table in the kitchen was a bouquet of radiant tulips, violets and lilies. Without thinking, I ran to the table to read the card that was attached. They were from Claudia. I was a little disappointed because a part of me wanted them to be from Eric, but I really appreciated Claudia's kindheartedness. She had already done so much.

The sound of the toilet flushing stirred me, and I turned around, eager to thank her for the flowers.

"Oh hi, Sabrina. I didn't hear you come in." Silvia walked into the kitchen.

"Hey. Yeah, I just got here."

"We never really got a chance to meet. I am Claudia's sister, Silvia Hernandez," she said, holding her hand out.

I shook it and smiled at her. She was a tall, thin, good-looking woman with blonde highlights in her hair that looked like they needed a touch-up. I could tell she was younger than Claudia, but not as pretty.

"A pleasure to meet you, Silvia. I didn't even know that Claudia had a sister," I replied, looking through the cabinets for a wineglass.

"Yep. The one and only. She's my big sister."

"Is she here?" I inquired.

"No. She left for work right after she came in this morning."

"Oh, okay. Would you like a drink?" I offered her as I presumptuously removed two glasses.

"You don't think it's too early? What are we drinking?" she asked, pulling out a chair to sit at the table.

"Ever heard of *After Shock*?"

"Aye, yi, yi! That's too potent for me. You have anything that isn't as strong?"

"What do you want? I'll make it for you."

"Is it true? How about a Pina Colada?"

I made a face, shook my head and suggested something else.

"Usually that would be no problem, but right now that's a bit too much work for me. I'm sorry, only quick fixes today. How about a White Russian?"

"I never have it, but since you make, I try."

It took me less than two minutes to fill my glass with the pink liqueur, and stir up her glass of Baileys and milk, with a smidgen of *Absolut* vodka for a little zing. It reminded me of my old days at Elektric, that dreadful place where I met Eric. Now I rue the day.

I sat in the chair directly across from her. Silvia guzzled the drink like it was water and laughed when she saw the surprised look on my face. I laughed out loud in response, then tossed back my glass of liqueur and immediately felt it go straight to my head.

"Bravo!" she exclaimed, clapping her hands together. "Again, yes?"

I liked her. She was definitely different from Claudia, more of a firecracker. I didn't know the whole story between her and Claudia, but I couldn't imagine her hurting her own sister. Then again, it's the people who are the closest to you who hurt you the most. I have definitely proven that one, time and time again.

"Yeah, let's do it!" I began to make the same drink for her, but this time she held my hand just in time before I poured the milk.

"No milk this time, eh, and just a little bit more vodka." Silvia winced as she demonstrated what "just a little bit" looked like by bringing her thumb and index finger close together, without them touching.

"Then you might as well have what I'm having. The effect is the same," I replied, as I poured myself another.

"Oh, no, I don't drink like that anymore. I'm trying to cut back, you know. This is nothing, believe me. This little drink won't have any effect on me, but what I want to know is what effect are you going for?"

"Look." I lifted the bottle to make my point. "I'm trying to get through the after-shock of my whole life crashing before me, and this little pink potion is going to help me to do that."

I made hers the way she requested and gulped my drink so fast it burned like fire going down. I thought I could feel the hairs growing on my chest, and my head got even woozier.

"Ugh! This drink is no joke. One more!" I proposed.

"No, no, gracias. I stop here."

"Suit yourself," I said, adding another fill to my glass.

"So, are you going to tell me what happened?"

Boy, she was nosy. "I'm sorry, Silvia. Maybe another time. I really don't feel like talking right now, especially about my drama. I just want to sit here and enjoy my drink. I hope you don't mind."

She smiled and nodded sympathetically, as though she understood where I was coming from. I didn't know this woman from a hole in the wall, and although the liquor put me in a lively mood, I did not care to share my personal problems with Silvia.

"So, where are you from, what brings you to New York, and how long are you here for?" I asked, deliberately trying to change the subject.

"Bogota, Columbia, born and raised. It's a lovely place and I think you would like very much. As for New York, I used to travel back and forth to buy merchandise for the jewelry store I used to own; *La Bella's Jewels.*" She giggled after she quoted the name of her store.

"But anyway, when *my* life got out of control, the very person I hurt the most was the only one who helped me. It's my own fault I suppose, but like my mama used to say, 'bueno o malo: tu recibe lo que tu cosecha.' In English it means, 'good or bad: we always reap what we sow'."

Although Silvia's accent was extremely thick, her English was not bad at all.

"Yeah, what happened?" I was just as inquisitive as she had been, and I quickly caught myself. "I'm sorry, I don't mean to pry. You don't have to answer that."

"Oh, please. I don't mind. I've put Claudia through a lot of pain because of my own selfishness and I'm here to help her out in anyway I can. I'm not sure if she has told you, but several years ago, I fell in love, or in what I thought was love, with Claudia's husband, Ramon Payala. I actually seduced him, and after a long affair he finally left my sister to be with me. Not long after, we wed. Shortly after the marriage began, Ramon started to beat and rape me, and eventually destroyed everything I had worked so hard for. He ruined my livelihood and almost my life. But the worst part in all of this was realizing just how much I hurt my own sister. Can I have another drink, please?"

Intrigued by her story, I rose to make her another White Russian. I staggered a bit at first but quickly found my balance. As I made the drink, she continued.

"I know you want to ask me why I did what I did, but there is no real answer. I still ask myself everyday. If I say, I was just selfish and self-serving, would it be enough? Or maybe it was just that I was jealous of what Claudia had and wanted it for myself. I don't know the answer, Sabrina, but I know that Claudia's forgiveness is something that I still can't understand."

I handed her the drink and stood with my back against the counter. With my arms folded, I listened intently, trying hard not to judge her. The tears welled up in her eyes.

"I don't think I would be capable of doing what she did. A love like that makes me want to change my life and be a better woman, and sister. Claudia says she wouldn't change the past if she had a choice, because after everything happened, that's when she met Jesus. Can you believe it? Now, I've never been the religious type, quite the opposite. But let me tell you, I really think there is something real about this. Not like the Roman Catholic stuff we were brought up believing. I can't explain it, but I'm definitely open to learning more about the Jesus who Claudia talks about. And let me tell you something else, for *me* to say that, means that I have come a long way."

"Wow!" was all I could say. I mean, that was an incredible story; and the way Claudia conducted herself, you would never be able to tell that she had gone through something so extreme. Silvia laughed out as she wiped her tears with a napkin on the table.

"Yeah. Wow!" she chimed in.

☾ • ☾ • ☾ ☾ • ☾ •

I wasn't nearly as drunk as I hoped to be, but I was feeling quite tipsy and very disinterested in just being in the house. With renewed energy, I decided that I needed to go out to clear my head. If I stayed indoors, I would go batty, thinking about Eric and Monique and these babies I was carrying. Silvia wasn't interested in doing anything but staying in.

I thought about calling Erica. This was the first time we had ever had a falling out. I know she did what she felt was the right thing. Was it really fair to expect her to choose between her twin brother and me? I would have done the same thing for Melvin if the shoe were on the other foot. I was just so hurt and embarrassed. In spite of her choice to keep her brother's dirty secret, I still loved her and wanted us to remain friends even though Eric and I were through.

Her phone rang out and went to voicemail. I didn't leave a message. I would call her back after taking a well needed shower. Silvia offered to clean up the mess in the kitchen, and I headed for the bathroom to freshen up.

The thirty-minute shower felt great even though it brought down my buzz. Before putting on the clothes I had laid out on the bed, I stood naked in front of the full-length mirror behind my bedroom door. I looked for any evidence of pregnancy, turning this way and that, rubbing both hands repeatedly over my belly. Had this been a year ago, I would be in sheer bliss. But it wasn't and I felt so cheated. Bamboozled and hoodwinked by the ones closest to me. But, I still loved Eric. A part of me wanted to forgive him, but I was torn. My mind was telling me "No!", but my heart was telling me "Yes." He wasn't sure about how he felt about us as a couple anymore, and I can't even bear the thought of being number two in his life.

The alcohol had me tripping because I suddenly felt the urge to call him. I fought to dismiss the thought, snapped myself back into reality and proceeded to get dressed. What I needed to do was be at Planned Parenthood by Monday to see about the abortion. *The quicker, the better,* I thought.

From the kitchen, I could hear the familiar ring tone of my cell phone that I had left on the table.

Eric! I wishfully thought to myself.

I hurriedly gathered the towel around my partially nude body and made a mad dash out the door and into the kitchen. I almost fell and broke my hip as I lost my footing running out of the room. Silvia was done in the kitchen and had retreated to her room. Frantic, I grabbed the phone and flipped it open before identifying the caller.

"Hello!"

"Hey, baby. How are you doing?"

I looked at the phone. It was a Georgia number. I recognized the voice.

"Hi, Gina. What do you want?" I didn't try to hide the disappointment and disdain in my voice.

"Why must you always be so disrespectful, Sabrina? I'm your mother; don't be calling me 'Gina.' Have some respect, child." My mother snapped at me.

She was funny because I never recalled her being much of a mother to me, and as far as I was concerned, she was not deserving of my respect.

"What can I do for you, *Mother?*" I said sarcastically.

"I don't know why I bother with you..."

"Look," I interjected, "do you have something to say, because I'm in the middle of something and I don't have time to bicker with you."

She hissed her teeth. "I'm calling because your grandmother is very sick and she's been asking for you, okay?"

I pulled out a chair to sit. "What happened?"

"She's been in and out of the hospital for the past month, but she told the doctors that she don't want them running no more tests on her. She made them send her home, but she's not doing well at all. The cancer is taking its toll on her. She's been asking for you, and I think you ought to come see her real soon."

"All right, tell her I'm coming and that I said to be strong and hold on."

"When you coming?" my mother inquired.

"I don't know, Gina... I mean Mother, but I'll be there as soon as possible, okay? I have to go now. Thanks for calling. Bye."

I hung up the phone and sat, dazed, in my chair. I was scared. I didn't want my Grandie to die. Cancer was a deplorable enemy, and I hated it in every way, shape and form. The disease had ravaged my grandmother's liver for the past five years, leaving her thin, bald and ailing. She had put up one hell of a fight in the beginning, using chemotherapy, various medications, and prayer to beat the cancer into remission, but the disease spread so rapidly that Grandie soon gave up.

"What ever happened to 'by His stripes you are healed'?" I would provoke her. I wanted her to keep up the fight.

"Let the Lord have His way, Sabbie," she would say. "His will, not mine, be done."

But I knew it was her way of surrendering to the lashes of cancer, and I resented God the more for allowing her to go through so much pain and suffering.

It had only been one year since I lost my brother and she was the only person left who truly loved me, and on whom I could completely depend. I didn't waste any time. I ran back to my room to pack a suitcase. I was going to Georgia immediately.

Chapter 9

There was no way I could afford to fly out to Georgia tonight. After just losing my job and Eric, I was forced to be more conscious of my spending habits. No airline, with the exception of Northwest, charged less than nine hundred dollars. They offered a discount rate of five hundred and thirty four dollars but I would be subject to two connections and an overnight layover. Not even the cheap-fare websites provided reasonable fares, most likely because of the last-minute booking. The prices were exorbitant and it didn't make much sense to go with either of those options. So, I decided to drive.

Every trace of alcohol in my body was gone. The news about Grandie sobered me up quickly. I needed to do whatever was necessary to be with her and there was no use in sitting around the computer waiting for ticket prices to drop.

With my bags packed and ready to go, I wrote Claudia a quick note and attached the ten dollar cab fare I promised to repay. Just as I went to give the envelope to Silvia, I heard the sound of a key rustling in the front door.

"Hey, Claudia," I said, backing up to greet her as she stepped inside. "I was just about to leave a note for you."

I handed her the envelope.

"What's this?" she asked looking at it as if it were a mystery.

"I have to leave town tonight. I have an emergency back home."

"Sabrina, is everything okay?" She always came across as so sincere. "How are you feeling? I wanted us to sit and talk a bit."

"Well, it's not what you think. My grandmother is very ill and I must go to her. She needs me, and I need to be there for her."

"I'm so sorry to hear that. You poor dear, you've been through so much. What time is your flight?"

"I'm actually going to drive down instead. Last minute thing, you know."

"But your car's not here."

Oh crap! I forgot that I had left my car back at Eric's place. There was just so much on my mind.

"Man, I completely forgot, you know, Claudia. I left my car in the Bronx. You know what, I'll just call a cab."

"No, I'll take you!" Claudia exclaimed, helping me with one of my bags.

I tried earnestly to dissuade her. She had just come in from a long shift at work and I knew she was tired. Silvia had been waiting for her all day and here Claudia was, tending to me again. She insisted it was no problem, and was determined to have her way. I had to admit that I was glad to save the extra twenty dollars for gas or toll. Eric's house was located in the Pelham Parkway section of the Bronx, and it was about a twenty minute ride from Harlem.

"I feel bad asking you to do this Claudia, but thanks a lot. Thanks also for being so good to me last night. You didn't have to go as far as you did and it really meant a lot to me."

"First of all, you didn't ask me. I offered. And secondly, you are more than welcome, and I don't want you to mention it again. Deal?"

I snickered and said, "All right, deal."

"Let me go and say hello to Silvia and get out of these work clothes, and then we'll go, okay?"

"Yeah, sure. Take your time, and maybe you can ask her if she wants to come along for the ride so you don't have to drive back alone."

Claudia went to her room to change and came back alone. Silvia was asleep. Must've been all those White Russians. Claudia grabbed one bag, I took the other, and we walked out the door.

As soon as we pulled up to Eric's street, I had Claudia drop me off a few houses away because I didn't want to draw attention to myself. She asked how I planned to carry all the bags for half a block by myself. When I could produce no viable answer, she suggested that I go for my car and then come back.

The night air was frigid and since the car had not been driven for a few days, I knew the engine would be even colder. Walking up to the entrance of Eric's house, I noticed that his Lexus was parked on the street. I was thankful that he didn't block my car in the driveway. From the front I could see that the house was practically in darkness, except for the dimmer light in the living room.

Curious to see if he was home, I tiptoed around the side of the house to see if the light in the bedroom was on. It was. Suddenly, the motion detector turned on, shone the bright light right where I was standing. I felt like a deer. I immediately froze with fear.

I totally forgot about this stupid light! Eric just had it installed a few weeks ago when some kids trashed the yard because he didn't have anything but fruit to give for Halloween.

Knowing he would come to look out the window, as he always did when the detector was triggered, I ran for cover behind the side of the above-ground pool. With my eyes shut tight and my teeth piercing into my bottom lip, I crouched down as low as I could, hoping and wishing the light wouldn't reflect on my pink bubble jacket, easily identifying me.

Maybe this was the real definition of *Crouching Tiger, Hidden Dragon*.

"What is it, Eric?" I heard Monique ask.

"Nothing, probably just a cat or a skunk. C'mon, you ready to go. I'll take you home now," he answered.

Aw hell! I have to get out of here before they see me. How embarrassing would that be? The light remained on; it was set for five minutes and I didn't want to take a chance on moving. Then again, I didn't want Claudia to come looking for me either. My heart was beating very fast. I felt pathetic, stooping so low. Like a moron, I had left my phone in her car and couldn't alert her.

Against my better judgment, I decided to wait it out. I figured if I made it out, they would realize that I was the culprit to set off the detector once they didn't see my car anymore. I didn't want to be seen as some crazy stalker. I just sat tight and wished even harder that Claudia would stay put.

The minute I heard Eric's car drive off, I emerged from behind the pool. My entire body was so numb that I could no longer feel my fingers or toes. I think it was more from the harsh realization that Monique had now assumed my position in Eric's life than the cold night air, and it hurt. I didn't even wait to warm up the car before screeching out of the driveway to meet my roommate up the street.

"I was getting worried, Sabrina. What took you so long?"

"Be easy, I'm fine. I had to warm up my car," I lied.

"Oh, okay. I tried to call you but it started ringing in here." She laughed out. "I was just about to come and get you, but thank God you are all right. Come on, let me help you."

After closing the trunk, Claudia handed me back the ten dollars I had placed in the envelope and told me to use it for gas. She moved over to where I was standing and told me to call her when I arrived and got settled. Then she asked if she could pray with me for safe traveling. I really didn't want to offend her, but I also didn't want to be subjected to any religious antics either. Letting her down as easily as I could, I asked her to say one for me while she was driving back, because it was getting so late, and I needed to get a move on.

She looked as though I gave her the response she expected. She then stepped in closer and hugged me; it was so weird. I was rarely ever affectionate with my own personal friends, and here was this woman who I barely knew embracing me like we were friends for years. I liked Claudia. There was something peculiarly genuine about her, yet I remained hesitant to reciprocate or fully accept her graciousness.

Tapping her gently on the back, I pulled away and thanked her again for everything she had done. Then, I jumped into my warm car and headed for the I-95 South.

Chapter 10

Fifteen hours. That was the estimated driving time from New York to Georgia that Map Quest had published on their website. But I had always done it in twelve, with the help of cruise control and a radar detector, of course. I had driven down south a few times and still kept the directions in my glove compartment. This, however, was the first time I was doing it by myself because Monique usually drove with me. I dug further in the glove box to make sure the detector was there. I never used it in New York, and I hadn't seen it in awhile.

It was not there. Then I instantly remembered that Niqi had borrowed it several months back when she drove up to Boston to visit her cousin. She was always taking my stuff and never returning anything without me having to ask her to return it. It figures. I should have seen it coming. That was just another indicator that she was designated to represent the Judas in my life, and I hated her so much now. Now, because of her, I had to be extra watchful of the speed limit and those pesky state troopers, especially on the Turnpike.

Traffic was smooth and I was able to drive nonstop for a little over four hours before pulling into a rest stop. I was hungry and definitely needed a cup of Joe for a quick pick-me-up. The only thing that kept me going for so long was the reggae and hip-hop CDs I had booming in the car.

McDonald's, TCBY and Pizza Hut Express were my only choices. Naturally, I opted for a Mickey D's extra value meal, classic fish filet and fries with black coffee. As I sat to down to eat, my phone rang.

Butterflies immediately invaded my stomach when I saw Eric's name light up the screen. I became so nervous that my mind went blank.

Should I, or should I not, pick up? The debate roiled in my mind before I finally decided.

"What do you want?" I answered, trying to sound impassive.

"Hi, baby. I miss you."

My heart melted at the sound of Eric's voice. When I didn't respond, he continued.

"Can you come back over here? We need to talk about this." My eyes widened and my jaw dropped to the floor.

"What are you talking about?" I said, trying to keep it together.

"I saw you outside my window a while ago and that's why I made her leave. I bought you that jacket, remember? I'd know you anywhere, Bri."

What could I say? I was busted.

"Whatever, Eric. That was nearly five hours ago. And for the record, you didn't *make* her leave, you *took* her home."

"Yes, I know. But that's because I wanted to see you, and if you won't come back, then I'm coming over there."

"Where? I'm not home."

"What you mean 'you're not home'? It's past midnight. Where are you?" he questioned, obviously taken by surprise.

"Eric, in case you didn't notice, when you decided to play house with my best friend, you lost the right to know my whereabouts. Besides, it's none of your concern. Look, I'm busy right now and I have to go, so see ya when I see ya."

"Bri, wait..."

Bye, Eric.

I closed the phone and then immediately wished I hadn't hung up on him. I was torn. On the one hand, I wanted my man back. I wanted to forgive and forget that this whole thing ever happened. I wanted to get on with our plans to get married and have our twin babies, the way it happens in the romance novels and soap operas. But on the other hand, I refused to wait for him to decide what he wanted by going back and forth between Monique and me.

I wasn't going to play number two to any woman, especially not Monique Henry. It looked as if he had already made his choice and now, whether I liked it or not, I was forced to make mine. Now, all I had to do was find a way to deal with it and move on. Easier said than done.

Now, because of Eric Morrison, I had lost my appetite. I wrapped up the fish sandwich, dumped the rest of the fries, and downed the last of the coffee. I filled up my tank at the gas station behind the restaurants and continued on my journey.

♩ • ♩ • ♩ ♩ • ♩ •

Driving through the night and into the morning, I saw the sun come up. It lingered beautifully on the darkened horizon before it gradually penetrated the dawn. At this time of night I would normally be turning over in my bed. If it wasn't for the consoling vibes of Mary J. Blige, Jill Scott and Kelly Price, I doubt I would have been able to make it this far.

♪ *"She was a friend of mine, she left with my man, she lied, cheated, took all I had..."* ♪

Man, Kelly really understood my pain.

With so many hours of driving still ahead of me, listening to the all these sad songs got depressing after awhile. There was only so much I could take and then no more. All I did was think about Eric and Monique.

Why would they do this to me? How could they do this to me? What were they doing now?

They were both responsible for the hole in my heart and I was left alone to deal with it. I only wish that heaven could lend me my brother for one more day.

Melvin would have known exactly what to say to help me get through this dilemma. He was used to me sobbing over guys that had hurt my feelings and never failed to give me his male insight to get me through the situation.

"You gotta leave these toads alone and wait for your prince, Bri-Bri," he told me once during one of my heartbreak dramas. I had to laugh. He had this amazing gift to make you laugh even though you wanted to cry. I desperately needed him now.

The sad part was Melvin really liked Eric. They got along well. He said I had snagged a good one, and that Eric might be the prince he had said would come. Mel would have been so disappointed to see how badly Eric had betrayed me.

As far as Niqi was concerned, Mel just tolerated her, because she was my friend. He didn't see why we were friends and was sure it wouldn't last.

"She's not like Courtney," he had said the day he met Niqi. That really irritated me then. It was easy for him to say that, though, because he had a major crush on Courtney. She could do no wrong in his sight.

Courtney, Courtney, Courtney! I knew just how Jan Brady felt. I was so tired of hearing how great Courtney was from him and my grandmother. They swore up and down that Courtney Wallace was perfect. I won't lie; at one time I used to think so too.

We had been friends since the third grade and were totally embedded into each other's family. It was as if her parents were also mine and my grandmother, hers. We were like sisters. She was so cool and funny. That girl would make me laugh everyday. She had that mischievous edge to her that kept you coming back for more.

One of my fondest memories of her was in the seventh grade when she had her first Spanish class. Walking home after school one day, she came up with this crazy idea to make some money.

"Watch this," she told me. I stood off to the side and watched as she walked up to the first Hispanic man she saw.

"Hola. Como esta?"

"Hola," the man replied, looking at her strangely.

"Puedo tener un dolare, por favor?"

With the same look of confusion and without saying another word, he reached into his pocket, handed her a dollar and walked off.

Completely impressed, I ran up to her and asked, "What did you just say? How did you get him to give you a dollar?"

"I asked him to," she said, shrugging her shoulders.

"Teach me!"

That was the start of something beautiful. We each took turns doing it and made out with about six dollars each. We did it everywhere, almost every day, sometimes walking away with a twenty dollar jackpot for the day. The men were always more giving than the women. Women usually asked too many questions.

One day we made the mistake of propositioning the wrong person: Clarice Wallace's hairdresser. Courtney's mother loved going to Olga's Beauty Shop, and they all knew her very well. I don't think Courtney recognized her, because when she asked Olga, who spoke perfect English, the lady was nice enough to give her the money. The next time Mrs. Wallace went in for her wash and set, Olga tattled like a parrot. She made it seem so much worse than it really was. Olga told Court's mom that she had seen her daughter begging for all sorts of money from everybody on the street. Courtney's mother was so embarrassed and angry that she put Courtney on punishment for two whole months; no TV, no going out, no company.

I couldn't even go over to their house. The only time we saw each other was in school and when we walked home together. Needless to say, that was the end of that ruse. Courtney was so dismayed by the severe punishment that the only Spanish she used outside of school was when she went to Taco Bell.

The wily side of Courtney's personality didn't fully cease to exist, however. By the time eleventh grade came around, she had learned a new trick. When I reminded her of the seventh-grade experience, she confidently stated, "That was an old-rip off scheme; this, my dear, is work. We'll be earning this money."

Our new "job" location was at the mall and we worked the three to four o'clock shift everyday after school. At first we started with other high school students, then the security guards, and finally, anybody who would give us their attention.

"How would you like it if we read your mind?" Courtney would propose.

"Excuse me? How do you plan to do that?" the unsuspecting person rube would ask.

"Okay, here's the plan. If I can read your mind, you give me fifty cents. If I can't, my sister and I will give *you* a dollar. How does that sound?"

For most participants it sounded like a pretty good deal, because they sincerely believed that there was no way this girl was going to read their mind. Or so they thought.

"Okay, I want you to tell my sister a word, any word you can think of and I'll guess it." Courtney walked away, far enough so she could not hear what the person said in my ear. As soon as she came back, we would start the game.

"Snaps is the name of the game, feel the vibes!" we would chant together and wiggle our fingers in each other's face as a mode of emitting some mystical vibe. I looked deep in her eyes and began.

"**M**ommy said we should be home early today." I snapped my fingers four times and continued.

"**V**icky is having a party on Saturday." I snapped my fingers three more times, and then twice more.

"**S**orry for making you late today."

"Movies!" Courtney hollered. She was right on, and our recruit would be amazed at how we did it. By the time they tried to figure it out, we got our money and went on to the next person.

"Don't you know it's time to go home?" One, two snaps.

"Never cross the street without looking both ways."

"Zoos are fun places." One, two snaps.

"Let me help you with your homework."

I pause for a second and wiggle my fingers at her to indicate that there was a second word.

"When are you going to study for the test?" One snap.

"So how about those Knicks?"

"Homework sucks." One, two, three snaps.

"Natalie is..."

"Denzel Washington!" Courtney blurted out, before I was finished. And again we were paid.

We had so much fun doing it and most people were good sports. Sometimes they tried to up the ante to two dollars by giving harder words like supercali-fragilistic-expiali-docious which was really stupid because by the time I got to s-u-p-e-r, Courtney pretty much had it figured out. That was common.

Every once in awhile we would lose a challenge when she got presumptuous about a word. Like the time somebody gave me the word *superhero* and she guessed *su-*

percali-fragilistic-expiali-docious. Or if some brainiac gave a word that either I couldn't spell or she didn't know, like *assiduous* or *perspicacity*. We hated those, but it came with the territory. It was, as she would say, "Most times you win, sometimes you lose."

Courtney used to be a lot of fun back in the day, but she changed so much when she found religion. At first, it was cool. I respected her decision to change her life for the better, but after awhile she just took it too far. Although church was never really my thing, most people I knew only went on Sundays. Courtney went three, and sometimes four days out of the week. There was Sunday service, Prayer meeting, Bible study, Convocation, Revival... She hardly had time to spend with her friends. It was just ridiculous.

She stopped coming with me to the clubs and even scrutinized the movies she went to. When "*Dracula 2000*" came out, I begged her to come with me to see it. It was my treat and she still turned me down. Horror flicks had never been a problem before. Courtney kept giving me some lame excuse about opening doors to her spirit and the need to guard her ear and eye gates. Crazy! She tried her best to make me understand where she was coming from, but the way I saw it, she had just lost her damn mind.

Soon enough, our relationship just slowly waned. Fewer visits turned into fewer phone calls, and in time we simply grew apart. Moving to New York was an opportune excuse, but the truth was we had stopped being friends long before that. The last I saw her was a year ago at Melvin's funeral, and we barely spoke even then. Sometimes I miss what we had, but the old Courtney was gone and I really didn't like the new one all that much.

☾☽ • ☾☽ • ☾☽ ☾☽ • ☾☽ •

I drove for six continuous hours, thinking about my old friend, and hoping I wouldn't run into her during my visit. Before I knew it, the pangs of drowsiness soon began to overwhelm me. Slowly but surely, I could feel the weight of sleepiness bearing down on my eyelids. I tried jerking back and stretching my eyes often in a futile attempt to remain alert. It wasn't until I heard the frightening sound of my tires going over the jagged bumpy edge of the highway that I finally jolted into full consciousness. Determined not to die or kill someone else in the process, I cautiously drove two miles to the next rest stop and dozed for about an hour.

By the time I woke up, it was a little past seven-thirty. I wanted to be in Georgia by at least noon. I drove to the next gas station convenience store, grabbed a Red Bull, sunflower seeds to keep me busy, and some Nacho Cheese Combos. I filled up again at the Sunoco and drove on. According to the signs on the highway, I had about 211 miles left to go, and it seemed that I would make it to my destination in the set time.

Chapter 11

Three gasoline refills, two Carolinas and one more Red Bull later, I finally crossed over the state line of Georgia. The one thing I missed about this state that New York lacked was the sixty-five degree weather in late November. A gentle breeze wafted, making it feel like a sunny autumn day in September. Although they had changed colors, there were still leaves on the trees.

Some people were out walking their dogs, while others strolled with their Bibles in hand, on their way to church. Young kids rode their bicycles up and down the sidewalks, as adults tended to their yards, gardens and cars.

I love New York, but Georgia has no slushy snow and plowing to contend with every winter and no need for oversized bubble coats. All you need is a cute leather jacket and you are good to go. Besides my grandmother, the climate was the only thing I missed about this place.

My car pulled up in front of 13 Millstone Place at exactly twenty-eight past eleven in the morning. This was the first time I had come back here since Mel's funeral a year ago. I always needed to prepare myself mentally before setting one foot into this house. I swear, if it weren't for my Grandie, these people would never see or hear from me.

The minute I walked through the squeaky black metal gate, the abscence of Melvin's presence was almost tangible. The once blossoming garden that lined Grandie's porch was now fruitless and barren. There was no life left in the beautiful sunflowers and tulips that had once added such beauty to the yard. The tomatoes, peppers, eggplants and squash we harvested during the fall, usually in time for Thanksgiving, were completely dried up. All that was left were the withered remains that hung flaccidly on twigs.

When Grandie got sick and was no longer able, Mel tended to the garden. Now it was a perfect symbol of his absence in our lives. I truly believe that if it weren't for my careless mother and her reckless choices, my brother would still be here today. Every now and then the fresh hard feelings rise to the surface of my heart to remind me that I am still bitter.

The drizzle on my head quickened my pace and I was relieved that I had avoided driving in it. I ran to the side of the house to find the spare key to the front door. It was still in the same spot it had been for years, tucked discreetly in the ear of the ceramic dog that sat on the lawn.

☾ • ☾ • ☾ ☾ • ☾ •

For as long as I can remember, Pamela Richards always kept her house the same way, year in and year out. She had always been a stickler for fresh flowers in the foyer and the living room. Her favorites were lilies and tulips and, on occasion, red and white roses. Grandie usually kept one bouquet on the piano at the side of the stairs, and another on the coffee table. Once a week when she would come home from shopping for groceries, she would send Mel and me to unload the car and pack them away.

Neither one of us was allowed to touch the flowers, as it was her pleasure to set them just the way she fancied. It always gave the house such a fresh, cheery feeling, that no matter how bad my day had been, walking into the house made me forget what ever had gone wrong. Looking back, I can't say it was the flowers, more than my grand-mother's love, that made all my troubles disappear. Just having Grandie around made living in this house more bearable, even after Gina brought Doomes to live with us.

Calvin Doomes is by far the worst human being on the face of the planet. Gina brought him to live with us when Mel and I were just twelve years old. I never knew why Grandie allowed it, but the day he came with all his bags, I knew all hell was going to break loose.

"C'mere Bri, I want you to meet somebody very special," my mother had said the Sunday afternoon she brought him home.

I turned around suddenly from the piano to see my mother standing in front of the stairs with her newest friend. I didn't move a muscle.

"Don't be rude, Bri. This is your new daddy, Uncle Calvin. C'mon over here."

She walked over and pulled me off the piano bench, by my arm, forcing my feet to shuffle over to the giant stranger she called my "daddy".

He was a big, burly black man with a major resemblance to Ving Rhames, but without the bald head. His black and orange nylon convertible jacket was way too small for him, and all he wore underneath was a gray v-neck tee shirt with a hole in the neck. This had to be the fifth or sixth "uncle" we had met in the last year, and I prayed this one would leave just as quickly as all the others had. The thing that made this time different was that out of the many priors, Doomes was the only one to actually move in. This worried me.

"Hey gal, good to finally meet ya! I have been hearing a lot about ya. C'mere and give your new pappy a hug. You're a pretty lil' thing. Just like your momma."

He always chuckled after every sentence he spoke, like a big stupid hyena.

Ugh! He smelled like roach spray and malt liquor. As he grabbed me, my arms hung listlessly by my sides. Pulling myself away with a scowl on my face, I made it perfectly clear that I did not appreciate his affection.

"Where's your brother?" Gina asked excitedly, as if Doomes was a trophy she couldn't wait to show off.

"He's at church with Grandie."

"Oh, that's right," she recalled. "Well, why you not there with them?"

"Because I was tired!" I said tersely.

Slap! That was the sound of the back of my mother's hand across my face.

"Don't ever talk to me like that again. You hear me, little girl?"

"That's the way to do it baby," Doomes said, and then he chuckled. He picked my mother up, threw her over his shoulder like a sack of potatoes and carried her up the stairs.

"Let daddy show *ya* how proud *ya* made him."

Gina started laughing and squealing like some silly schoolgirl as he carried her away. With my lips quivering, I stood there in total shock, my hands on my throbbing jaw, as the tears rolled down my face. She had never hit me like that before and certainly never in front of anyone. That was just the beginning of the worst to come.

Even now, standing at the bottom of the same stairs some fifteen years later, the memory was still fresh in my mind. Now, however, there were no more freshly cut flowers anywhere, only an old dusty futon that replaced the piano. Something told me that it was one more of Grandie's many favored possessions that Doomes made Gina sell.

Climbing up to the second floor, I noticed that the crystal chandelier and oil paintings were also missing. I wondered how long they had been gone, and whether Grandie knew that my mother and her boyfriend had stolen and hocked all her valuables.

Grandie's room door was ajar and although I didn't want to disturb her, I peeked in to make sure she was asleep. The squeaking of the door stirred her, and as I backed out to leave, she called out for me.

"Sabbie?" She was the only person I allowed to call me by that name. "Is that you?"

"Hi Grandie, yes it's me. I'm sorry to disturb you. Go back to sleep. I'll be here when you get up." I always reverted to the little girl of yesteryears in her presence.

"Nonsense, child. I've been waiting for you, and I knew you would come. Get here next to me."

She spoke in a soft gentle whisper as she sat up a little and patted the side of her bed. Her voice was shaky, but she seemed comfortable, even though the cancer had been weakening her body with each passing day.

I ran to her, my eyes filled with tears. The once robust and beautiful Pamela Richards was now a gaunt, feeble, aged woman. There was a catheter in her arm and an oxygen mask over her nose. She removed them both when I came in. She usually kept her head wrapped because the chemotherapy had stripped every bit of her beautiful hair. But now that it was uncovered, I could plainly see the bald patches on her scalp. Nevertheless, she was still *my* beautiful grandmother and despite her appearance, she was completely lucid. For this, I was grateful.

I removed my shoes and climbed in the bed with her as I did when I was a child. Even though I had my own room, Grandie never allowed me to sleep there. My room was solely for doing my homework, playing with my toys, and storing my stuff. Only every so often, if I had a sleepover, would we be allowed to sleep in my room. Other than that, Grandie's bed was where I slept every night until I was about sixteen years old. It was a little bizarre, but I just got used to it after awhile. It was a very safe place for me, and those are some of the memories I still cherish.

Here again, in this haven, I held on tightly, getting as close as I could, to my grandmother. I wanted to etch this moment forever in my heart. Deep down I knew my time with her was short, so I wanted to savor every hour, minute, and second that we were together. Just having her loving arms enfold me, transformed me into that vulnerable little girl I used to be. It never failed. Grandie always had that effect on me and being with her now triggered the emotions I wanted to suppress, and brought back the reality of the past two days.

"Are you all right, Grandie? Am I hurting you?" I wanted to be sure that she was just as comfortable as I was.

"I'm fine, Sabbie, but I can tell you're not. Tell me, what's wrong?"

I did. I told her about everything that had happened in the last few days; well, almost everything. I told her about Hilton and how he had so shamelessly fired me, about seeing Monique and Eric together, the files I found in his office, and Erica's knowledge of the whole thing. I even told her about the confrontations with each of them, and Monique's pregnancy.

But I didn't tell her about mine. What was the point? I already intended to make an appointment at the clinic in Atlanta tomorrow anyway. And besides, Grandie hated abortions and would have strongly opposed my decision.

"Good Lord, Sabbie. Eric? The same Eric you're supposed to marry next year?"

She looked stunned and confused, and took her time to push herself up further in the bed, as though that would give her some clarity. I nodded and pouted like a seven-year-old little girl instead of a grown twenty-seven-year-old woman.

"And Monique? The two of you used to be so close. What kind of friend would do such a thing? You know what I think? Courtney would have never done that to you. Now, she was your true friend, but you walked away from her, Sabrina. You abandoned that friendship and all because she started going to church and changing her life for the better."

Here we go again...

"But Grandie, she..." I tried to defend myself, wanting the chance to explain.

"No, Sabrina, listen to me. Sometimes hardships and trials come into our lives when God is trying to get our attention. Trust me; I've been there. You have been through a lot. Hell! This whole family has, but it's not until we each turn to God that our lives will properly fall into place."

"Really, Grandie," I said condescendingly, "like Mel's did, right? His life fell properly into place too, huh?"

"Don't be snide with me, young lady," she shot back, and coughed harshly.

"Sorry, Grandie." I rubbed her back and she nodded to show that she was fine.

"Sabrina, there is a lot you don't know or understand and unless you let go of that bitterness and learn to forgive, your life will always be in a mess. You need to confront those demons from your past and you cannot do that unless you learn to trust God. You always harden your heart when we talk about this, but you need to listen. Mel was right with God when he died and although I don't understand everything, it was God's will. Who are we to argue with that? We may not always agree with God's point of view, but we must accept it. We have no other choice, because His ways are not our ways, nor are His thoughts our thoughts. Are you hearing me, child?"

I nodded and she resumed.

"Now, I'm not condemning you and I hate to say it, but I never trusted that girl Monique. She seemed nice and all, but I didn't get a sense of genuineness from her. Not like Courtney. I bet you didn't know that she and Mel had gotten very close. They were planning to get married."

"What!" I got out of the bed and walked around her room in disbelief. "What! When? How?" I repeated, sounding like a broken record.

Courtney Wallace and Melvin Richards; they sounded like words that didn't belong in the same sentence. I knew that they had continued to be friends when she and I stopped, but romantically involved? I couldn't grasp it. I looked at Grandie.

"Oh, I don't remember any dates, but it would have been some time this year. They still remained friends when you moved to New York, and used to converse regularly when he started going to Clark. Courtney invited him to her Bible study once and Mel couldn't get enough. Shortly after, Mel gave his life to the Lord. He got saved and it was all he talked about."

Grandie smiled as she reminisced about her only grandson. "He fell in love with Courtney in no time, and then *she* was all he talked about. He was so happy." She laughed at the memories.

"Wow! Why didn't anybody ever tell me? Why didn't Mel tell me?" I questioned her.

"He wanted to wait for the right time. Because of the way you had left things with Courtney, both of them wanted to wait until the time was right. Every time you came home, you always stayed in a hotel. If my memory serves me right, this is the first time you've been back since you left eight years ago."

"No, Grandie. I was here for Mel's funeral, remember?"

"Yes, but that was only for the wake and you only stayed in the house for fifteen minutes. Then you, Eric and Monique went back to your hotel. Right after the funeral ended, you all went back to New York."

Looking through her bedroom window I saw that the rain was coming down really hard now. What could I say? She was right. I couldn't stand to be around my mother any longer than I had to. She was the reason Melvin was dead, I wanted nothing to do with her, and I still don't.

After Doomes came to live with us, my mother's behavior changed drastically. She had always been a bit of an erratic woman, but at one time I could always count on her being there. But that was so long ago, I think I just made that up. Gina was a beautiful woman and I can't recall there ever being a time when a gentleman caller wasn't hovering over her. She was always energetic, with a wry sense of humor. In other words, she spoke her mind even when the timing wasn't right. But it was what the fellows loved most about her, and it kept them coming back for more.

All except Doomes. He had a different effect on Gina. I really don't know how long they were seeing each other before he came to Grandie's house, but nothing was ever the same after that.

Maybe a month or so after he moved in, my grandmother started to constantly complain that her money and other valuables had gone missing from the house. First it was small things, like five or ten dollars, then quickly, larger bills too would disappear.

Next the blender and the juicer went missing, followed by Grandie's favorite silver cutlery and the TVs. Even her hubcaps and two rear tires mysteriously disappeared from her car, one time. One by one, the items in our home were being auctioned off to the highest bidder.

Every now and then I would hear Grandie yelling at my mother saying, "Gina, I don't want that stuff in my house! Are you forgetting you got kids here?"

"What about me, Ma? Remember what happened to me?"

"Keep your voice down," Grandie would say, and then back off.

How I used to wish then that I could be the one to put it to my mother. There would be nothing she could say to me that would ever make me back down. But I was only twelve and when I would ask what they were arguing about, Grandie had a clever way of making everything seem as though it was not that bad, like she had everything under control. Then one unexpected day, Mel and I discovered what "that stuff" was.

It was a spring afternoon in mid April and we had come home early from school. As we opened the door, Mel and I entered the house quietly. At that time, the basement was the designated place for the family to relax, play or finish any homework we had. Grandie had furnished it with a TV, video games, a bookcase filled with books and a stereo, most of which were eventually stolen by one or two members of the household.

Assuming she was upstairs sleeping, we headed straight to the basement, taking extra care not to wake her. If the truth be told, we eagerly wanted to finish a Zelda video game we had started the day before, and we didn't want to do our homework first. When we reached the bottom of the stairs, we carefully dropped our bags and rushed to the Nintendo. We weren't there for five minutes when I heard voices coming from the bathroom.

Unnerved and panicky, I put the game on pause and tiptoed to the bathroom. When I pushed the partially closed door, I saw Doomes and Gina smoking crack!

The only reason I knew what it was, is because I had just seen the movie *New Jack City* a couple of weeks prior. Doomes held a smoke-filled glass container to my mother's mouth as she inhaled the filthy substance.

There were four small glass vials strewn on the floor and two red lighters. I gasped at the top of my voice and Mel rapidly came running up behind me. Instinctively, I pushed him back, trying to protect him from seeing what they were doing. It was the worst, most shameful thing I had ever seen in all my young existence.

"Oh, *sh...!*" my mother cursed after removing her mouth from the glass pipe.

"Close the door, you little maggot!" Doomes howled harsh profanities at me, and it scared me so badly that I slammed the door, pulled Mel by the arm and ran upstairs to Grandie's room. She wasn't there.

Neither Gina nor I ever said a word about that day. Doomes, however, made it his duty to remind me to keep my "mouth shut and just forget about what you think you saw."

Believe me, I have been trying ever since.

"You listening to me, child?"

"Hmm, huh! Um, yes Grandie." I shuddered at the recollection. "I'm sorry, could you please repeat that?"

"I said that I don't want you to torture yourself about Monique and Eric. Just leave them to God and time. What they have done cannot prosper and their relationship will come to nothing. Come here."

She tapped the side of the bed once again, and I sat next to her. Cupping my face gently in her hands, she looked into my eyes and spoke firmly.

"You will not let this break you down, because what doesn't kill you only makes you stronger. You are a resilient child, you've always been, and you will get past this. *The darkest part of a night is just before the dawn,* and your dawn will come. I promise you that."

She released my face and I lay down with her, yet again. Those were the very same words Melvin had said in my dream. I wept bitterly for my losses. Mel, Eric, as well as Monique, and in a short while, my two innocent babies, and possibly, even Grandie.

The tears were so heavy they soaked right through her shirt. Still she held me close to her, stroking my hair as she used to, until my body was completely relaxed and we both finally fell asleep.

Chapter 12

The piercing sirens of several emergency vehicles passing by roused me at around six thirty. I was surprised that I had slept for so long, but after all that driving, I was completely worn out. Moving with caution as I shifted out of her bed, I tried not to stir Grandie.

Tiptoeing out of her room, I moseyed out into the hallway. Lights were turned on throughout the house and voices were coming from downstairs. But I really didn't feel like seeing anyone, not yet. At that moment I wanted only to get back in bed with my grandmother, but did not want to wake her. She needed to rest in peace.

Heading down the hall in the direction of my old room, I suddenly felt compelled to enter Melvin's instead. It had been eight years since I last stepped in his room. It felt so surreal. Everything was different from the last time, but it felt and looked like he still slept here.

Mel's room was clean and his football medals, plaques and other accolades were all dusted and organized. From the numerous trophies displayed on the shelf, I picked up the one he most valued. Directly next to it on the wall was the enlarged laminated newspaper article featuring him and his college team. He had smiled so big for the camera and his eyes lit up like a twinkling star. Looking at it now made me smile to think of how happy he had been that day.

That was only two years ago. I had dragged Monique with me to visit him at Clark Atlanta University for their homecoming weekend. He was a sophomore and an all-star player for the college football team. The Championship game at the Georgia Dome was the big event on campus, and all throughout Atlanta, that weekend. Everybody, including the local news and members of the press were in attendance.

Over twenty thousand people filled the arena. They were scattered throughout the Dome, which could hold up to thirty thousand. The atmosphere was rowdy, as supporters for each team shouted and rooted for their players, waving flags and pom-poms, blowing whistles and foghorns. Monique wasn't a big sports fan, but I knew the game well. I constantly had to explain to her when our team did something worth cheering.

I was so proud of Melvin. His position was wide receiver and he was doing his thing out there on the field. This was what he dreamed of all his life. He wanted to go pro. Recruiters were always checking him out. Melvin Richards' name was on the "hot prospects list" of the most popular sports agents. I just know that if life had taken a different turn, my brother would have made it to the big leagues.

... ten seconds left in the game, no more timeouts, the ball is on the Panthers 45-yard line. The score is 21-20, Panthers down by one point. The center snaps the ball to the quarterback. He backs up as six defenders dash toward him on the blitz. He sees Mel down the field at the 25-yard line and manages to throw a long pass to him. As Mel catches it, he looks up into the crowd at me and mouths, "This one's for you, Sis." He shakes two defenders, breaks a tackle, and runs into the end zone to score the game-winning touchdown. The crowd goes wild!

There was no need to explain to Monique this time. She definitely got the picture. We went insane, screaming until we were almost hoarse. Melvin, with his crazy self, holds on to the ball and did the same dance as Ray Lewis from the Baltimore Ravens. Mel's teammates rush him and they too get crazy, dancing, whooping and hollering with elation. That was the game that crowned Melvin Richards MVP of the Clark Panthers. We celebrated hard that night.

I really miss those days and miss my twin brother even more. Now, here I am, sitting in his room, on his bed, reminiscing about his life. There was so much more we had planned to do in this life.

Damn, here come these tears again.

As I turned to lie down, hoping to feel a little closer to him, I heard a faint tap on the door. I looked up, perfectly disappointed to see Gina pop her head in.

"Good, you're up. Hi." She walked in, carrying a tray with a plate of oxtail and rice with mixed vegetables, and a glass of Cranberry juice. "Miss Maxine cooked and I figured you might be hungry. I peeped in on you sleeping next to Momma, but I didn't want to wake you. You been asleep a long time. What time'd' you get here?" she jabbered on before finally taking a breath.

"Miss Maxine is here! You made her leave Grandie in the house all alone?" I complained, immediately trying to find fault.

Brazenly, I sat up and took the tray from her. I don't even think I said "thank you." Oh well...

The food looked divine and I knew it would taste even better. Mel used to rave about how much of a great cook Miss Maxine was. Both he and Grandie adored her. They were convinced that she was a chef in another life. She was from Jamaica and had been Grandie's live-in attendant for the past five years. I didn't know her that well, but Mel sang her praises. We must have met only once or twice but we spoke a lot about Grandie's health almost every time I called.

Mmm, the food was good.

"We went to church, Bri. We go the same time every Sunday. Momma knows. She insists on it and will raise hell... oops! I mean, get real mad if we don't go."

"Church! *You* go to church?" I almost choked.

"Yes, I go to church," she said, hoisting both hands to her hips. "Every Sunday now for the past seven months. Yes, ma'am."

I stopped eating and took a good look at the woman standing in front of me. *Regina Richards Goes to Church...* now, that's headline news for you. I couldn't fathom the thought, and for the first time I was speechless. There was something peculiar about her, now that I examined her more closely. She looked clear, tranquil even; then it hit me. She was sober! I had not seen my mother so completely lucid in years.

The glow that surrounded her made her look beautiful. I had forgotten how pretty she was and could feel a tinge of tears starting. I forced myself to squelch the urge.

"I'm a changed woman, Bri," she said proudly.

I gave her that *I've-heard-that-once-before* look, but she continued.

"No, it's true. I'm not the same person I used to be. God has given me a second chance to make some things right and I plan to take it."

She moved toward me and knelt down. I thought she was going to start praying or weirding out like Courtney used to do.

"What are you doing?" I asked, obviously confused.

She took my hands and looked at them as she resumed.

"Sabrina, I love you. And I realize that I have done a lot of stupid, selfish things in my life, things that I'm not proud of. But worst of all, is how I have not been there for you or Melvin, and I'm sorry." She looked into my eyes. "I know I have hurt you deeply and I acknowledge my failure as a mother, and I humbly ask you to forgive me."

The silence was deafening. I couldn't believe my eyes or my ears. I really believed for a second that I had somehow entered the twilight zone. This was too much to take. My heart began to soften a little toward her when my leg nudged Melvin's trophy that lay next to me. When I glanced at it, anger resurfaced. I pulled my hands away from her and picked up my plate to continue eating.

"Forgive you?" I asked, chewing and talking at the same time. "Forgive you for what? What exactly are you asking forgiveness for, Gina? I'd really like to know. Is it for bringing Doomes into our home, and allowing him to treat your kids like "flowers in the attic", and ruining our family? Or maybe for stealing all of my grandmother's money and valuables, my clothes, my toys, or my savings?

"No, maybe you want forgiveness for putting my grandmother under so much stress and nearly killing her a few times. No, I know, it's for Melvin. You're the reason he's dead, you know? Oh, let's not forget the times we had to see you smoking that junk. And all the fights we had at school because those kids were always teasing us about our 'base-head mother'. Shall I go on, because I've got more, Mother. Is that what you're asking forgiveness for?"

She was crying a river through her eyes and nose, but never stopped to wipe her face.

"Yes," she whispered, "and a whole lot more. Sabrina, there is a lot you don't understand or know about, and if you'll just give me a chance and hear me out, I'll explain right now."

Still eating, but a little intrigued, I retorted. "Say what you have to say, Gina. But I really don't see how it's going to change anything."

My mother got up from the floor, pulled Mel's desk chair closer to the bed and sat in front of me.

"Look, what I'm about to tell you is not an excuse for my actions, but I think it might help you to understand why I was so unstable."

"That's putting it mildly," I scoffed.

"Be that as it may... As you already know, Momma and I didn't always used to live here in College Park. We lived in a little apartment in Atlanta with Pete, my stepdaddy. He died before you were born. Well, Pete used to drink like a fish almost every night, and then he would let your grandmother have it. He would beat her so badly, sometimes she wouldn't leave the house for days."

I looked at her with skepticism, wondering if she was telling me the truth.

"Oh, yes," she continued, as if she could read my mind. "She's not like that no more, but it's true. Anyway, by the time I was fourteen, Pete started coming into my room late at night when Momma was asleep. At first he would just feel on me, in all my private areas, and then he would make me feel and put my mouth on him. When he got bored with that, he just started raping me. I was about fifteen by that time. I used to protest at first, trying my hardest to fight him off me, but it was useless. He was too strong for me.

"After awhile I stopped objecting and just got used to his nightly visits. I didn't say nothing about it to nobody for a long time, because I had grown so terrified of him. I knew how vicious he was with momma and I didn't know how far he was capable of going. I was a young girl and Pete took advantage of that. For a long time, I felt like Momma already knew because he didn't beat her as much anymore, and I kind of resented her for it.

"So anyway, one night Pete came home rip-roaring drunk as always, and started in on Momma because she hadn't finished cooking dinner yet. He started slapping her on the back of her head with a rolled up newspaper, taunting her while she was standing over the stove. He was so cruel. Momma just cried. That's all she ever did. She wanted to fight back, but he was much bigger than she was. Not to mention, she was also terrified of him.

"I don't know what got into me that night, but I had had enough. I couldn't stand to hear her bawl anymore. I didn't know what to do or say, but I just got up from the table where I was doing my homework and walked into the kitchen. I was trembling with every step, you could hear the fear in every word I spoke. 'Pete, please leave Momma alone. I'll let you do what you want to me. I promise I won't fight. Just leave her alone, please.' I begged him, hoping it would be enough to make him stop."

Gina squeezed her eyes really tight and started shaking her head, as if the memories she dredged up brought back more than just emotional grief. Her tone changed drastically, tears flooding her face and shirt. Her voice got more aggressive as she continued.

"I was just a little girl, Sabrina! He raped me over and over again for years, and I was just a little girl. I never wanted to tell Momma about the rapes, but I was so scared, and I just wanted him to stop hurting her. I remember my heart was beating so fast and my voice was just trembling as I tried to protect her. Right then and there, something in Momma just snapped. Momma snatched up the butcher knife from the counter and charged at him. 'You son-of-a...! Have you been in here molesting my daughter?'

"Her eyes were wide, her lips were tight, and she was fuming with rage. I really don't think that she was afraid of him anymore. Pete jumped back with fright and started hollering. 'She lying, Pam! What the hell wrong with you? Put that damn knife down.' It was a complete role reversal, and Momma was the one in control now.

"He turned to face me and started stammering. 'Now, you know I ain't never done nothin' to you. Why you try'na upset your momma, sittin' there tellin' 'em lies on me?'

"Momma looked at me, and I don't know what she saw, because I never said another word. She put the knife down on the counter, looked into Pete's eyes and vowed, 'I'm going kill you.'

"He left that night and didn't come back to the apartment for a whole week. Momma let him back in and acted like that night never happened. Sabrina, I tell you, it was so creepy. She just didn't talk as much, not even to me. Then a couple of weeks later, we got a call that Pete was dead. The doctors said he suffered from respiratory failure when he was at work. Something didn't seem kosher about the whole thing; it was just too convenient. But I never asked any questions and Momma never said anything about it.

"After the funeral and everything, she cashed in on his life insurance, bought this house, and we moved out here about two months later. Not long after that, we discovered that I was pregnant," Gina paused for a moment, then reluctantly continued, "with twins."

"What the hell did you just say?" I whispered. Shock engulfed me, and I came real close to regurgitating my dinner. "You're a damn liar, Gina! Are you trying to tell me that my grandmother's husband is my father?"

She swallowed hard. "*Was* your father; both you and Melvin. And as it turned out, Momma did follow through on her threat."

"What are you talking about?" I asked, not really wanting to hear anymore of her unbelievable tale.

"She killed him, Sabrina; and she did it for what he did to me."

"Oh, my God, you are *such* a liar! You need help, Gina, and I hope you find it."

I stood up to leave.

"Sit down!" she strictly commanded. "I am not finished, and I am not lying. I am telling you the truth. So whether you believe it or not, you are going to hear it."

Resentfully, I heeded and returned my backside to the bed.

"Why do I have to? I know my grandmother, and she would never do anything like that," I defended Grandie.

"Maybe not now. But that was nearly thirty years ago, and she was a different woman back then. I swear that I am not lying to you, Sabrina. Momma even confessed the whole thing to me four months ago. She was in the hospital then. I was reading the Bible to her one night, and in the middle of a scripture she just started to tell all.

'Regina, do you remember that week after Pete left the house?' I put the Book down, took off my glasses, and said, 'Yes, Momma'. Immediately, the butterflies began to flutter and my heart started to race. I had a feeling about where the conversation was going.

'Well, I knew he would come back sooner or later, especially for his medication. I had spent the week partially emptying his blood pressure capsules and refilling them with boric acid. When he finally came home, I acted like normal and just waited for him to collapse. God forgive me, but I killed that bastard and never had any regrets. Regina, you were exposed and subjected to a lot before you were old enough, and for that I'm sorry. I have always known that the reason for all your problems with drugs and promiscuity was because of the personal and sexual abuse you suffered at the hands of Pete. Now, by no means am I trying to make excuses for how you have lived your life, but I understand why certain things happened the way they did. It's really amazing to see you finally turn your life around. God is good, and I thank Him every day for letting me live to see it. I love you, Regina, and I didn't want to die without you knowing the truth.'"

Gina stopped talking and looked at me for a reaction. Her story infuriated me.

"I don't believe a word you are saying. This must be your new and improved way of copping out of what you've done and placing the blame on other people. *Now*, all of a sudden, you want to talk about who our father was! Some drunken, deranged, wife-beating *rapist?* Oh, this is good, even for you, Gina. You are a piece of work, you know that. I don't believe a word, not one word, of what you are saying."

"I wouldn't make up something like that. It did happen. I am trying to own up to all the wrongs I have done in the past, and you deserve an explanation as to why I did a lot of the things that I did. I was pretty messed up after that; mentally, emotionally, you name it. I realize it's…"

I had to cut her off. I stood up and headed for the door.

"I don't want to hear anymore from you. You are a liar, you've always been, and I won't sit here and…"

"Think about it," she continued, stopping me in my tracks. "Why do you think she never let you sleep in your room when Calvin came here? It's because she didn't want to run the risk of the same thing happening to you. She was so guilt-ridden for so many years about what Pete did to me, and I never made it easy for her. Do you really think she would allow Calvin to live in this house and put up with all the junk we put this family through if I weren't manipulating her? I'm not proud of it, but I'm trying to be honest with you, Sabrina."

We were both crying vigorously now. I didn't want to believe her. How could I believe this atrocity? Storming out the door, I called out for Grandie. She would set it straight and brand Gina the liar she is.

"Grandie! Gran, wake up." Sobbing uncontrollably, I stood over her, gently trying to nudge her awake. "Grandie, please wake up, it's important."

No movement.

"Gran. Grandie?"

I must have called her name and shaken her countless times before realizing that something was wrong.

I screamed out for Miss Maxine. She rushed up the stairs and into the room, Gina trailing in behind her. Breathing heavily as I stepped out of the way, Miss Maxine moved in closer to examine my grandmother, checking her heart and lungs.

Not even a minute passed before she softly put down Grandie's hand. Carefully removing the stethoscope from her ears, she looked at me and slowly shook her head, confirming the worst.

"I'm sorry. She's gone."

"No-o-o-o!"

Chapter 13

Gina's story replayed over and over in my head as I rested in my grandmother's bed. I barely got a moment's sleep last night, sitting up thinking about this outrageous ordeal. For most of the night I stayed with my grandmother, fully aware that in a few short hours the morticians would come to take her away to the funeral home. This was the last time I would lie down by her side ever again. As her lifeless body lay in her bed, it seemed as though she was only sleeping, finally attaining her everlasting peace.

Even though she was gone, she looked like the victor over her five-year battle with cancer. The disease had lost, because it no longer had any control over her suffering. Surprisingly, I was not as upset over her passing as I had once believed I would be. Grandie had passed into eternity and though I know I'll miss her dearly, the thought of her and Mel together now was immensely consoling.

I had spent a lot of last night willing Grandie to wake up one more time, just to set the record straight about Gina's story.

Was there any truth to it?

Could Peter Randolph really have been my father? At one time Mel and I used to be so curious about him. All they ever told us was that he had died of a heart attack before we were born. My mother never, never once would give us a straight answer about him.

"Do you have any pictures?" we would ask.

"He didn't like taking pictures. Go clean up your toys," she would quickly change the topic.

"Were you and Daddy in love?" we would ask.

"Love is for fools," she would retort.

"Where did you and Daddy meet?" we would ask.

"Stop asking about him. Will the two of you please just leave the past in the past? Just leave it alone," she would demand.

She never gave us a real answer. After awhile, Mel and I just granted her request. We stopped asking about our phantom daddy.

And Grandie! Could she have really murdered her own husband? It sounded so fantastic! Now that she was gone, I wondered if I'd ever know the truth.

Funeral arrangements had already been made and Gina woke early to call and inform the undertakers of Grandie's passing. Since I hardly slept throughout the night, I stirred easily when the doorbell rang. I rose from the bed and went straight downstairs, following a few feet behind my mother as she answered the door. I went into the kitchen where Maxine had already made coffee.

"Good morning, gentlemen. Mr. Henderson, Mr. Warner," Gina said when she opened the door.

Two tall men, one black and one white, were standing there, dressed in black suits and hats. I recognized them as the same men who had worked on Melvin's funeral. The white man, who was puffing on the last of his cigarette, tossed it away and exhaled the smoke the moment he saw my mother. I could tell he wanted to get rid of it before she opened the door, and she caught him off guard. He seemed a bit embarrassed that she had seen the cigarette.

"You know, Mr. Warner, those things can kill you," Gina said candidly.

"You're right, Miss Richards, but at least I got Jim here to take care of me when I'm gone." He slapped the black guy on the back and chuckled loudly.

"Good morning, Miss Richards. How are you feeling this morning?" the black man, James Henderson, said. "We are truly sorry for your loss and want to assure you that we will do all we can to make your mother's funeral arrangement as smooth and comfortable as possible."

"Thank you, both. We appreciate that very much. Come inside, please."

She moved aside and the men entered the house. It was truly surreal to see her being so congenial and well mannered. The woman I knew would have flung the door open and probably said something like, *"Well, it's about time y'all got here."* What a difference a year makes, huh!

"Gentlemen, this is my daughter, Sabrina." She reintroduced me to the men when I entered the living room where they were all seated. They both rose to shake my hand.

"I remember. Good to see you again, Sabrina," Mr. Warner said.

"We're sorry for your loss," said the other man, as he released my hand.

"Thank you. Would any of you like a cup of coffee?" I offered, trying to be hospitable.

"That would be good, thank you," Mr. Henderson answered for both.

I left the room to prepare the coffee while my mother completed the funeral arrangements with the undertakers. After they were served, I excused myself and went back upstairs to check my voicemail. I wanted to see if Eric had called and was quite satisfied to hear his eighteen-second message checking up on my whereabouts.

I called him back almost immediately to inform him about Grandie. He offered his sincerest condolences and asked to be reminded of the correct address so he could send flowers.

Were flowers Eric's only solution to my pain and suffering? Not once did the jackass offer to fly down to be with me. I really needed him to be by my side at a time like this. That's when it really hit me that everything between him and me would now be final. There was no more chance of reconciliation. My next call was to schedule an appointment at Planned Parenthood. In spite of Grandie's passing, I still didn't want to delay the inevitable. The clinic in Atlanta was the only one with an opening for that afternoon, and I made sure my name was on their list.

Claudia had also called to confirm my safe arrival and left a message telling me that she was giving a month's notice on the apartment. Now that Silvia was permanently here, they needed to find a place with more space. I called her back right away.

"You know what, Claudia," I said, "there's really no need to rush, and since I don't know exactly when I'm coming home, Silvia is more than welcome to stay there. It's not a problem."

She thanked me, expressed her sympathy for the loss of my grandmother, and said she was praying for my family and me. Although it seemed like she wanted to, she didn't bring up the twins, and neither did I. There was already enough on my mind and I didn't want to be bombarded with any religious opinions on the matter. Besides, I doubted she could ever truly understand my plight.

☾ • ☾ • ☾ ☾ • ☾ •

"Sabrina Richards."

A short, chubby black lady holding a clipboard finally called my name. I sat in the crowded waiting room of Planned Parenthood for more than ninety minutes. It was about time. Why it had to take so long to be seen, only heaven knows. I walked through a door that led to the other side of the facility, where she directed me to a smaller room.

"Wait in there, and fill these out. Someone will be in shortly to talk to you," she instructed, handing me some forms. She then left to call the next name on her list. *Great, even more waiting.*

♪ *Murder she wrote, la da da, Murder she wrote…* ♪

The old reggae tune played from the overhead speakers in the room. I hissed my teeth at the would-be omen, and convinced myself that it wasn't murder; it was mercy.

Most of the wall spaces were covered with newborn baby-related posters. I had to wonder if this was an abortion clinic or a pediatric office.

There was a round blue formica table with three office chairs. Brochures of every kind were displayed in the center. I caught myself reading about Lamaze class, breastfeeding and even SIDS. Twenty minutes later, a Hispanic woman in a white coat entered the room with paperwork in hand. *Hilda Martinez* was the name engraved on a silver nameplate pinned to her coat lapel. I hurriedly placed the pamphlets back down on the table.

"Hello, Miss Richards. My name is Hilda Martinez, and I'm the Planned Parenthood counselor for the Atlanta office. May I call you Sabrina?"

"Yeah, that's fine. Um, no offense ma'am, but I don't need a counselor. I have already made my decision and now I'm here to proceed with the termination."

"I know, but this is the protocol we go by in this office. I just need to ask you a few questions. Is that all right?"

I nodded, completely annoyed by their stupid protocol.

"Great. How far along are you?"

"Eight weeks or so."

"Why do you want to have an abortion?"

I gritted my teeth before responding. "Because I'm not married, I'm unemployed, and I do not have the means to support twins at this stage of my life."

"Wow, twins, that's incredible! Congratulations. Sabrina, do you realize there are other options besides abortion?"

"Yes, I am aware. However, I am not interested in any other options. I know what I want," I retorted curtly.

"All right. How do you plan to pay for the procedure?"

Pay? I don't know why, but I was under the impression that it would be free.

"Well, how much does it cost?" I inquired.

"It all depends. If you had insurance coverage you would only pay the co-payment. But you indicated on the medical forms that you have no coverage, so you'll have to pay out of pocket. The full cost is, let me see…" She fumbled through the paperwork in her hand as if stalling for time, "Eight hundred and twenty five dollars."

Ouch. Abortions cost a lot of money, but what the heck, I needed it. I quickly contemplated my savings and concluded that even though it was going to be hard, it was also feasible.

"Okay, I can do it."

"Wait a minute." She removed a calculator from her pocket. "In your case the total is sixteen hundred and fifty dollars, plus tax, of course."

I looked at her as though she was crazy.

"Because they're twins," she clarified, holding out two fingers.

There was a moment of silence. I couldn't afford that kind of money. I had already invested nearly ten thousand dollars into the planning of the wedding and my savings account only had a balance of two thousand. If I had to pay for this procedure out of pocket, I would be flat broke and I still had to live and eat. I hadn't even gotten the bill from the Emergency Room in New York yet, and I know that that visit wasn't going to be cheap.

"Perhaps you'd like to consider those other options now, Sabrina. An abortion is not always the best route to take. As you can see, it's expensive, can have adverse effects on your body and your ability to have children in the future and, what's more, you could die."

My eyes widened.

"Oh, yes," she continued. "It is a surgical procedure and with any type of surgery, there is always a risk factor. Would you like to hear some information about adoption as an alternative?"

Forgetting her name, I glanced at her nametag. "Miss Martinez..."

"You can call me Hilda," she interjected.

"Okay. Hilda, I obviously cannot afford that type of money right now, and the thought of adoption has never appealed to me. I need to think about this, but I'll definitely get back to you."

"That's fine, Sabrina. Here's my card."

As she handed it to me, Grandie's smiling face flashed before my eyes. Hilda held onto my hand and said in a soft, familiar voice, "You ought to know that an abortion is a permanent solution to a temporary problem. And any problem you may be facing is an opportunity for Jesus to do something miraculous in your life."

Instantly, Hilda's voice returned to its normal tone. "Call me if you have any questions whatsoever."

"Thank you." I jadedly replied, shoving the business card in my purse.

I walked out of the clinic feeling even more confused and flustered than when I first arrived. That appointment did not go as expected. I was heated. Wasn't it against protocol for any professional employee to talk about Jesus? I could report Hilda for trying to impose her religion on me. I suppose she was only trying to help, but I really didn't need to hear her opinion on the subject of abortion. This was my business!

What in the world was I going to do now? I felt so powerless and alone. How the hell did my life turn inside out like this? A month ago everything was great, and now, nothing is right. I was an assistant manager of a popular clothing store. I had a wonderful fiancé who spoiled me rotten, whose family became mine. I had a sick, but living grandmother, a girlfriend who had my back, and a fabulous wedding to plan. Now I have nothing, and no one.

Where do I go from here?

Chapter 14

Atlanta's traffic was just as bad, if not worse, than New York's. It was only mid-afternoon and it was touch and go on Interstate 285. I understand why some people don't drive. It's just too congested. If I didn't already own a car, public transportation would suit me just fine. Driving at a snail's pace always drove me crazy. After twenty-five minutes, I couldn't take it anymore. Local streets had to be better. At the first opportunity, I moved to the extreme right lane and got off at the next exit.

At the end of the ramp were several orange-and-black detour signs posted about.

Alternate Route: COURTS STREET.

Ugh, what is it today with the redirection?

It took almost another twenty minutes to get back on the main road. I would have been home already had I only stayed on the thruway. Patience really is a good quality.

With all the construction going on, I hardly noticed that I had driven past Mayflower Avenue. For reasons unbeknownst to me, I reversed my little red Integra and turned down the lane where I had spent many a day running, skipping and playing as a child.

Two minutes later, I found myself standing at the front door of Courtney Wallace's house. Hesitant to ring the doorbell, I just stood there, contemplating about whether or not I should. No sooner than I was about to walk away, the door was flung open and there was Courtney, looking very surprised to see me at her doorstep. She was as radiant as ever.

"Uh, hi!" She was taken aback. "Oh my goodness! What an incredible coincidence. I was just on my way to Miss Pam's house to see you. Your mother told me what happened. Come here."

Courtney moved in to embrace me, and I hugged her back.

"Hi, Courtney," I said, as we let go of each other.

"Hi, Bri. How are you? Come inside."

I followed her as she led the way down to the basement. The place we used to hang out, play and watch TV was now a fully furnished and carpeted apartment.

Various Ethnic Art paintings adorned the walls. A curio filled with figurines portrayed African and Black American cultures. The living room was painted in a flat tan color, like that of a peanut shell, and one accent wall that popped with bright brick-red. The room was furnished with a brown, micro-fiber sofa and loveseat that complimented the color scheme perfectly. My favorite, however, was the brown and red horizontal pinstripe futon that tied the whole scene together.

Her place was nice with a quaint, comfortable feel to it. At the top of her entertainment center and on the windowsill were several pictures. A few of them featured photos of Melvin and Courtney together. I still couldn't believe what I had heard about them.

There was one with Melvin posing in his football uniform, and a couple with Courtney and the sixth-grade class she taught. The one that stood out the most was my twin, down on bended knee, holding a small jewelry gift box up to an astonished Courtney. It was a beautiful picture. The photographer captured so much in that microsecond of space and time. It was taken on a beach as the sun was setting, the wind blowing through her hair. My heart leaped at the image, and for a moment reminded me of my own similar proposal from Eric. How uncanny that was.

"It's a lot different down here now than it was when we were kids, huh, Bri?" Courtney said, breaking my concentration.

"Hmm...Yes. It's very nice, Court. How long ago did you remodel it?"

"Oh, boy. It's been well over five years now." She paused. "I'm glad you're here, Sabrina. It's really good to see you."

"Yeah, you too." I walked over to the window and picked up the picture that had stolen my attention. I turned to face Courtney and she smiled sweetly.

"Tell me about this, you and Melvin. I mean, if you don't mind me asking."

"Come over here and have a seat." She invited, as she sat across from me. She reached out for the picture and I handed it to her. "Well, after Mel started going to Clark, we would see each other around campus all the time. Even when we were growing up, it was no secret that he had a crush on me, but hey, that's what boys do, right? Anyway, he would call every now and again, and we would chat for hours. Sometimes we talked about you or your mom, or Miss Pam, and other times we just talked about nothing but life. Soon, he became interested in my lifestyle and started coming to church and Bible study with me. Not too long after that, he accepted Jesus Christ as his Savior and was born again. Within three months, he told me that he had fallen in love with me, and it wasn't long before I fell in love right back. It's really weird though, Bri, because for as long as I've known you guys, Mel was always like my brother, too. But he grew into such a charming, wonderful, Godly man. He became my best friend and we were inseparable.

"This picture was taken at Miami Beach. Joel James Ministries was hosting a Christian conference there one weekend. Our hotel was on the strip, and on our last day there, Mel asked to go for a walk on the beach. He told me how much he loved me and wanted us to spend the rest of our lives together. That's when he proposed. Another couple on the beach saw us, took the picture, and asked us for our address so they could mail it to us. Isn't that awesome?"

"Wow. Yeah, it is." I was still in awe over the whole thing. "What I just can't understand is, how come nobody bothered to tell me until now?"

"It's not that we didn't want to, but you were so aloof toward me; we just wanted to wait for the right time. I guess it never came."

Courtney rose from the couch and walked over to the window to put the picture down. She kept her back to me and gazed out the window.

"He loved you so much, Sabrina, and was so hopeful for the day you and I would be close friends again. We used to pray for you all the time. That God would watch over you and keep you safe from harm out there in New York, and I'm happy to see He did just that."

"Yeah, if that's what you want to call it. God hasn't exactly been on my side much lately, Courtney, so pardon me if I don't share your enthusiasm. No offense, but I don't think He was listening that closely to you or Mel."

She turned around briskly and faced me.

"What do you mean?" Her brow furrowed at my statement.

"I just don't share the same sentiment about God that you do. I think He's mean, and that He helps whomever He wants to, whenever He wants to. That's what I mean."

"That is not true, Sabrina. God is not mean. He is loving and faithful, and to prove it, look at what He did for your mother. Mel and I used to pray day and night for that woman. Now look at her. She is completely transformed."

"Oh, please! Don't tell me y'all bought her act!" I retorted incredulously.

"That is no act, Sabrina. That's God." Courtney spoke with conviction.

"Well then, why is it that God can turn my mother's life around, but He can't do the same for me? And if He is so good or *faithful*, as you put it, why did He take Melvin and not someone else who deserved to die."

She came back over to where I was and sat next to me.

"Look, Bri. I can't sit here and explain to you God's way of doing things. He has His reasons and I have dedicated my life to trusting Him. Mel did too. God's Word is the final authority on anything that concerns me, and if He does something we deem drastic, He is faithful to give us the grace to endure. I was devastated when I lost Mel. His murder completely tore me apart, and I questioned God until I was weak. And do you know what He said to me? *'For I know the plans I have for you. Plans of peace and not of evil, to give you a future and a hope, and an expected end.'* He also reminded me through His Word that, '*weeping may endure for a night, but joy comes in the morning.*' And you know what, He was right." She paused and giggled. "He's always right, Sabrina, and once you get that understanding, it's all uphill from there. Look at the work that has been done in your mother. Haven't you noticed the divine change?"

"Yeah, what a difference a year makes."

"No. What a difference Jesus makes," Courtney corrected.

"If that's what you want to call it, but she's the reason Mel is dead. Where was Jesus then?" I pointed out to her.

"Yes, to some extent. Jesus..."

"To some extent!" I echoed, cutting her off in the middle of her response. The details of my brother's murder were never my favorite topic of conversation and my nerves were beginning to get the better of me. I could feel my blood begin to boil and the veins in my neck throbbing. In my mind, there was no just cause for Mel's death. None!

"Mel is dead because of my mother and her crackhead boyfriend. That is a fact, point blank! That's why Doomes is serving a life sentence in prison, remember? I wish to God that they had given him the death penalty, but the part that gets me crazy, is that the bullet was meant for Gina. I'm not trying to wish death upon her, but Mel was the innocent one, and she should have never gotten him involved in her mess. She should have found her own way home and left him out of it."

Courtney remained calm. "Sabrina, in spite of everything, Mel loved his mother and he would do anything he could to help her. She needed him to pick her up that night and he responded out of love for her."

"Yeah, that's my point, and that love got him killed. Gina knew she should not have stolen money and drugs from Doomes. She knew how violent he was, and it was stupid of her to think that he wouldn't miss his stuff. He woke up and caught her right in the act. I'm sorry, but she's a stupid woman. Doomes had abused my mother many times before, for trivial things, and to this day she still has those scars.

"I'll never forget the time when he whacked her in the head with a beer bottle because she drank the last one out of the six-pack that *she* bought, out of which *he* had drunk four. She had to get like eight stitches to patch up that wound. I know you remember the time when he jabbed her with the butt of a lit cigarette, because she had smoked the last one out of the pack and didn't leave half of it for him. You can still see the burn marks on her arms, Courtney."

Courtney nodded at the memory.

"I mean, come on," I continued. "I don't know what made her think that he wouldn't do something worse if she stole his money and his crack!" I hissed through my teeth and fanned my hand to emphasize my disgust.

"I know, I hear you. They were both very high by the time Mel got to the motel. Calvin had already beat Gina pretty badly with the gun. Her face had been so severely bruised, and her arms and legs were bloody and battered. As soon as Mel got there, he just bum-rushed the room. There was crack and marijuana paraphernalia strewn all about. Calvin got very edgy when he saw your brother. He grabbed Gina and put the pistol to her head, she started screaming uncontrollably, and that's where everything started to go downhill."

"I wish Mel had just minded his own business. He would still be here today."

"Maybe, but come on, you know your brother. Mel had to try to talk some sense into Calvin. Mel tried to calm him down and get everybody out safely, but Calvin was so high that he wasn't rational enough to hear Mel. He was just yelling and screaming all the known obscenities about your mother - I won't repeat them - and that, nobody steals from him and lives. Melvin figured the best way to get out of this situation was to try and get the gun from Calvin.

"Someone in another room heard your mother's screams and called the police. When Calvin heard the sirens, that's when he got really anxious and pulled back the safety lock on the gun. His final word to Mel was that he would kill Gina and then himself and that's how it was all going to end. That's when Mel got nervous and decided the only thing left for him to do was to get the gun. He lunged after Calvin and during the struggle over the weapon, it was fired. Mel was shot in the heart and died a few hours later at County Hospital."

Courtney rehashed the incident to me like I hadn't heard it before. Even though they were both drugged up, Gina and Doomes' reports to the police were identical and the only reason they didn't fry him is because he confessed to my brother's murder. He was sentenced to twenty-five years to life in a Georgia State Prison. That bastard murderer will never see the light of day again.

The fury that had laid dormant in my heart resurfaced.

"You know what I'll never be able to understand, Courtney? When Mel was dying, probably fighting to stay alive, I prayed and asked God to save him. I mean, I literally begged God with everything I had in me. And you know what, He slapped me in the face. And I'm sure you prayed too, right? And what happened? Nothing! My brother is dead and the *same* God you say is so good and loving could have saved him, but chose not to. He let Mel die in a cold hospital room with a bullet in his heart!"

I didn't realize it at first, but my speech was precise and emphatic. Each word was cutting to make the point of how senseless and futile it was to pray to a God who did as He pleased anyway. I mean, what was the point? I strongly doubted that even Courtney could provide a worthwhile answer that would make me even begin to comprehend what she or Mel thought was so great about their God.

"Sabrina, do you hear yourself? You have managed to make this all about you. Did you ever stop to think for a second that maybe Mel wanted to let go?" She spoke tenderly and with care. "Of course I prayed for Mel to live and not die, and continue to tell the world about the goodness of God. Many people came together, praying earnestly and believing that God would give us a miracle. But when he passed, we realized that God had other plans. It doesn't mean that we should stop praying when things don't go our way. That's a self-indulgent perspective."

She had to be kidding! *'Self-indulgent!'* Who did she think she was talking to? The nerve of her. If this were her brother we were talking about, I wonder if she would be so flippant.

"Well, I'm happy that you are able to understand why this happened to *my* twin, but I don't and probably never will, so please excuse my ignorance and *self-indulgency*."

"Sabrina, I realize why you feel the way you do, but please allow me to try and explain something to you. As you already know, Melvin had a personal relationship with Jesus Christ. He was already saved, and God allowed Gina to live instead, so that she could have a chance to accept Christ and receive the free gift of salvation. If that bullet had hit Gina and she had died that day, where do you think her soul would end up? Not heaven, that's for sure. But Melvin is there right now, and so is Miss Pam. Your brother took that bullet for your mother so that she could have a chance to repent and change her life. Look at her now. She has been delivered from a fourteen-year battle with drugs, without rehab. She's been working full time at a shelter for domestically abused women and children for the past six months, and she is actively involved in the prison ministry at her church. Now, be honest. Knowing where your mother is coming from, does that sound like a deliberate choice or a coincidence to you?"

"Could be guilt," I said sarcastically.

"Well, it's not guilt. She understands very well what was sacrificed for her, and is so grateful that she didn't die in her sin and miss the opportunity for salvation through Jesus Christ. God knew the plans He had in this situation and, if He did it for Regina Richards, then certainly He'll do it for you too. Sabrina, I really don't know what you're going through right now, but no matter how awful you think it is, I know that God can and will work it out for you. You just have to ask Him. Sometimes when the storms of life blow our way, it's usually an indication that God is speaking and trying to get our attention. I really hope you listen to what He has to say." She tapped me on the leg, then got up and walked into the kitchen. "You want something to drink?"

Overwhelmed by her speech, all I could manage to reply was, "Yes, please."

It was the first time I actually felt something in me soften. Could there be any validity to what Courtney just said? It's not like she was pressuring me to convert or trying to convince me to believe what she did. She was only sharing the reality of who God is in her and my mother's life, and at one time, in Mel's.

I couldn't help the tears that streamed down my face, yet couldn't explain them. Before she returned with my cranberry juice, I tried to compose myself. I think she noticed the dried tears, because she asked me if I was all right. When I told her I was fine, she changed the subject, and we played catch-up.

Courtney told me about her parents' reunion after being separated for five years. They were planning a second wedding early next spring. We talked about her job, and how much she loved her students and being a teacher.

I was able to muster the courage to tell her about Eric and me, and our sordid break-up. Without going into too much detail, I explained that he had cheated on me with Monique and I had broken off the engagement. For fear of judgment, I didn't tell her about my pregnancy. She offered her sympathy and reassured me that everything was going to be all right.

From your lips to God's ears, I thought to myself. At least He listened to her.

Confrontation always made me nervous, but before I got up to leave, I made it a point to apologize for the way I had abandoned our friendship. I now saw how foolish and immature I had been to reject a true friend, and then accept a counterfeit one. Monique was no worse a friend to me than I had been to Courtney. We truly do reap what we sow, and it's unfortunate that it took such a painful situation for me to see that. Better late than never, though.

"You always were a very good friend to me, Courtney, probably the best I've ever had, and I rejected you because of your faith in God. It's just that you had changed so much, so fast; and at first it was fine but the more you got into it, the less important I felt. It sounds dumb, I know, but I didn't know of a better way to handle it than to withdraw from you. Looking back, I see how immature my behavior was, and though I may not have understood your faith, the way I handled it was completely unacceptable. I'm so glad that Melvin had the sense to maintain his friendship with you, and it would have been fabulous to have you as a sister. Courtney, I want you to know that I am very sorry, and hope you can forgive me." As nervous as I felt saying those words, I knew they needed to be said.

"I forgave you eight years ago, Sabrina, and you're already my sister. I'll always be here for you," she whispered as she embraced me again.

I believed her. "Thank you."

She walked me to the door and before I opened it, Courtney exclaimed, "Oh, wait a minute, I have something for you!"

She ran back downstairs and returned shortly, carrying a gray metal box. "Here, this is for you."

"What is it?" I asked, perplexed.

"Your grandmother gave this to Mel a few years ago. She wanted him to keep it in a safe place... you know, so that Gina or Calvin couldn't get to it. So he kept it here."

"What's in it?"

"I don't know. I never asked, and Mel never said. The keys are taped to the bottom."

I thanked her again and she hugged me for the third time. After that, I drove straight back to College Park. Strangely, there wasn't any more traffic or detours. Can't help but wonder if my little side trip had somehow been mystically arranged.

What a day!

Chapter 15

Funerals are usually depicted as melancholy, dreary ceremonies, but Grandie's Saturday afternoon memorial service was more like a homegoing celebration. At least, that was what her church sisters were calling it. I won't lie; it was a beautiful service and even though I will miss her very much, she is in a much better place now.

At my request, I harmonized, *"It's so Hard to Say Goodbye to Yesterday,"* by Boys II Men. I don't think Grandie's church sisters liked it that much, because when the song was over they all looked as though I had just sung something by the Back Street Boys... probably because it wasn't a Christian song. Well, I didn't know any songs about Beulah Land or going yonder to Zion, and frankly, I thought my selection was touching. It even moved some, including myself, to tears.

The morticians had done a wonderful job of making Grandie look natural. They managed to preserve the noticeable smile that was left on her face. I had no doubt that she would indeed rest in peace. The church was packed with Grandie's friends, neighbors, and church and family members. Courtney and her family also came, making it a grand total of at least one hundred and thirty-two. That's how many people signed the guest book. Unfortunately, we were able to accommodate only sixty of them in the house for dinner.

Almost every church sister had cooked or bought something, so there were a variety of snacks, food, juices and sodas. It was some good food, too, and in the two weeks I had been here, pregnancy had made me ravenous. There was no liquor though, because Gina was adamant about not having any in the house. Those who wanted to drink had to go to the store for their own, and drink it outside. Gina and Miss Maxine were running around trying to be of service to everybody, while the church folk insisted that they sit and take it easy.

There were pictures of my grandmother hanging all around, and a few photo albums were displayed for the family to view and reminisce.

The entertaining and socializing had been left up to me. It hadn't been that long since the house had been buzzing with so much excitement. Many of the people here had also come for Melvin's funeral, just over a year ago. At that time, I had not stayed long enough to catch up with any of them and, boy, did they take advantage of my presence now.

There were a host of cousins, great aunts and great uncles. I couldn't keep up with them and all their comments and inquisitions. I barely recognized or knew some of these family members, yet each one questioned me a little more than the last.

"Look at you, Sabrina. How's it up there in New Yawk?"

"Where that fine man you got? Why you ain't bring him with you?"

"You putting on some weight there, girl. But you're looking good though."

"When's that wedding of yours going to take place? You know how much I love weddings."

And so it went. I don't know if it was all the probing or the food that triggered the nausea, but I began to feel queasy after a while. It was a symptom that had been plaguing me every day for the past week. I excused myself from the crowd and hurried upstairs. I sat on the bathroom floor next to the toilet and threw up my dinner.

No pun intended but, I was sick and tired of this. I'm sorry, but these kids had to go and no matter what, I had to find a way to get the money for the abortion. The temptation to call Eric and ask him overpowered me, and I caved in. Almost two whole weeks had passed since the last time we had spoken. I finally managed to get in touch with Erica, but she kindly asked me not to get her involved with the drama involving her brother and me. She said she had requested the same of Eric and apologized again for offending me. Erica still wanted us to continue being friends, but she just didn't want to be put in a position where she had to choose between us again. I was mildly hurt, but I had no choice other than to understand and respect her position.

As much as I wanted to confide in her, it wasn't fair to use her as a sounding board during the fall out of two people she cared so much for. I was almost sure she must have heard about Niqi's pregnancy by now, but I didn't bother to tell her about mine. Even though it wasn't intended, I took it as the farewell speech to our relationship. And since she wasn't going to be an aunt to the unborn children I carried, I humbled myself enough to call Eric.

"Sabrina! Hi, baby. How are things with you?" He answered after just one ring.

"I'm good," I casually replied.

"That's good, baby. I'm glad you called. How was your grandmother's funeral?"

"You know, it was a funeral. What more can I say?"

There was an awkward silence before I conjured up the courage.

"Look, Eric. I really hate to bother you, but I kind of need your help."

I could feel him perk straight up and dedicate his undivided attention.

"Yeah, sure. Anything. What's up?"

"Um…" This was not easy. "Look, I need to borrow some money, but I promise to pay it back as soon as I start working again."

"How much do you need?"

"Two thousand five hundred." I bit my lip and cringed, hoping he wouldn't deny me or ask what it was for. It was more than I needed, but was a nice round number.

"Is everything okay?"

"Everything is fine. Can you do it? I mean it's all right if you can't 'cause…"

"No, no, no. I can do it. When do you need it by?"

"Yesterday. But how soon do you think you can get it to me."

"All right, let me see. I could wire it to your account, but not 'til Monday. The bank already closed for the day. You know how the Saturday hours are."

"Yeah, that'll be fine. You want my account number now or…"

"*Eric, are you coming? We're going to be late. Who are you on the phone with?*"

In the middle of my sentence, I heard a woman's voice resonate in the background. It took a second for me to recognize that it was Monique's. Eric answered her back, but I couldn't make out what he said because he obviously must have covered the mouthpiece of the phone.

"I'm sorry about that," he nonchalantly said when he resumed our conversation. He acted like his secretary had just interrupted him on a business call or something.

"You know what, Eric, never mind. I don't need your money. I'll find another way to get rid of these babies."

"What? Sabrina, wait..."

I hung up the phone and sat there seething. This time it wasn't a matter of being hurt; I was just pissed off. I vowed to change my number.

Two minutes later my phone started to ring. "What the hell do you want from me?" I hollered into the receiver.

It was Courtney. I apologized for my rude outburst and told her everything that had happened. It just seemed easier to tell her the truth over the phone than in person. Not being able to see her face helped. She was so caring and understanding of my situation.

She was one of the most sensitive people I knew, and I guess I had just forgotten that about her. I cried my eyes out once again, as I revealed every grimy detail of my disgraceful predicament. And I mean *everything*, up to and including Monique's pregnancy as well as mine. I even told her of my plans to abort. Surprisingly, she didn't say anything about that part. Her main focus was on me, ensuring me that I would, in time, find healing and relief from all of the anger and pain.

When I told her about what Gina had revealed about Grandie and Peter Randolph, she was just as shocked as I had been. She said she didn't think Gina would lie about something like that, but also agreed that it was a mind-boggling concept to think of my grandmother as a murderess. She said she would pray and ask God to bring truth and revelation about the matter

We talked and talked for hours, until the batteries in my phone started to chirp. I still can't understand how she got me to say "yes", but I agreed to go to church with her in the morning.

Hmph, go figure.

Chapter 16

Earth Changers Church looked more like a college campus than a house of worship. Courtney turned into the enormous parking lot and it took almost fifteen minutes before she was finally able to find a space.

The only dress I had in Georgia was the one I recently purchased and had worn to Grandie's funeral. Courtney assured me that they placed minimal emphasis on appearance, and that I could wear whatever I had. Most of my wardrobe was limited to denim, and she convinced me that it was acceptable to wear jeans to church. In a gracious effort to not make me feel out of place, she decided to wear jeans as well. I thought that was really cool of her.

This gigantic church was where Melvin had come every week to worship, and it felt good to be in a place that was very important to him. The sanctuary alone, named the Earth Dome, was a massive arena that looked like it could host the Oscars or Grammys. Church membership was over ten thousand people and what was even more shocking was that the pastor was a black man. Now get this. His name is Clifton Dinero, and he sure looked like he had lots of dollars.

Courtney told me that he has a nationwide television program, but I had never seen or heard of him. Maybe I should ask him for the money I needed for my procedure. Doesn't the Bible say something about giving unto others and you shall receive, or something like that?

Other than funerals, I hadn't been to a church service since the Japanese invaded Pearl Harbor. I wasn't even born yet, but it seems like it's been that long. I had never seen a church building this colossal. I had to wonder how many years it took for the building fund to save up enough for the down payment alone. Court said that they acquired it through much fasting and praying, and that it was now completely debt-free.

"That's incredible!" I said, as we walked into the sanctuary.

It was big and I must add, very beautiful. The décor was royal blue with hints of purple in the carpet and the cushioned theater seats. Other churches I had visited had those hard wooden benches, and unless you brought your own seat cushion or pillow, there was nothing to offer relief from the cramping you would experience in your rear end.

On the stage were modern instruments and huge speakers to amplify the sound in this great place. Attached to the wall was a globe that had the words **EARTH CHANGERS** imprinted in the center. It reminded me of the one in the movie *Scarface* that read **THE WORLD IS YOURS**. Above the speakers, on each side of the platform, were big TV monitors so people in the nosebleed sections could get a clear view of the stage.

The ushers who welcomed us were so warm and friendly. Even though there were so many people around, many of the ushers knew Courtney and went out of their way to greet her.

She introduced me as Melvin's sister and almost all of them embraced me and expressed their delight in meeting me. These were some happy people, and I questioned if they were always like this.

"It's just the joy of the Lord!" Courtney explained as we took our seats in the front.

Okay, whatever that means, I thought to myself.

Clifton Dinero is one handsome man, either in his late thirties or early forties. He walked assertively onto the pulpit after we had finished singing, and motivated his congregation to "Keep on praising the Lord. Come on, He's worthy to be praised! Hallelujah!"

Courtney and everyone else around me screamed and shouted exuberantly, while I just stood and clapped my hands. I don't know what it was about Pastor Dinero, but I liked him immediately. He had such a genuine, vibrant spirit that made you want to listen to every word he spoke. The topic of his sermon was, "Have Faith in God."

"Turn your Bibles with me, to Mark, the eleventh chapter. Look at verses twenty two and twenty three. When you find it, say, 'Amen'", Pastor Dinero instructed.

The pages of a thousand or more Bibles could be heard rustling through the auditorium, as parishioners diligently searched for the precise passage. Not even fifteen seconds had passed before there was a resounding, "Amen!"

Even though I had taken one of Grandie's Bibles with me, it was taking me a lot longer to find the verse. I honestly did not even know where to begin looking. Courtney must have detected that, because in the ten seconds it took her to find it, she handed over her black leather-bound Bible to me, with the scripture verse clearly highlighted on the page. She probably knew it by heart.

The reverend directed us all to read the passage together. "*And Jesus answering said unto them, Have faith in God, For verily I say unto you, that whosoever shall say unto this mountain, be thou removed, and be thou cast into the sea; and shall not doubt in his heart, but shall believe that those things which he says shall come to pass; he shall have whatsoever he says.*"

Pastor Dinero spent several minutes expounding on the scripture verses, and the relevance to our personal lives. He had my undivided attention when he explained that, "God does not respect people, but He respects principles and He respects faith. If we put our trust in Him, He will lighten every burden in our lives. It is strictly a condition folks; if we do, *then* God does. There is no problem you can ever have that is bigger than God is. Instead of telling God how big your problem is, why not tell your problem how big your God is? When you take this kind of attitude, you operate in faith, and your faith can move mountains, just as the Bible says it can."

Every so often, the congregation would respond with a unanimous, "Amen!" or "Preach, Pastor!"

"Church, there is power in the name of Jesus and when you give your life completely over to Him, that power immediately becomes available to you. Reading your Bible and praying every day helps us to grow in faith; because faith comes by hearing, and hearing comes by reading the Word of God. Think about the situation you are in right now, because everybody has a situation. Have you, in all your own might, been able to resolve the issue or find a way out?"

"No, sir!" yelled one congregant.

"Are you that self-sufficient that you can carry and cope with your own burdens, and do it without manipulation or taking shortcuts?" the pastor continued with his line of questions.

"Not me!" shouted another.

"I've never seen one person that is able to do it. Well, what in the world do you have to lose by giving Jesus the opportunity to turn your grief into joy? Let Him turn your mourning into dancing. The songwriter said it best, 'Oh, what peace we often forfeit, oh, what needless pain we bear, all because we do not carry, everything to God in prayer.' Come on now, my brothers and sisters, be wise. There is just no other way, but Jesus! He is the only way, and there is power in that name! Jesus. Jesus. Jesus! Hallelujah!"

As he wrapped up his message, the organist started to play a soft, soothing melody.

Pastor Dinero concluded, "If you don't know Jesus Christ today as Lord of your life, I urge you to come now. Life is too short, and tomorrow is not promised to any of us. While He's knocking at the door of your heart today, right now, invite Him in. He died to be with you. He died to be there *for* you in any situation you may be facing in your life today. Won't you come? Come to Jesus, He wants to heal you; He wants to save you and make you whole again. Come! He's waiting for you, come..."

At this segment of the service I began to shudder violently, as tears began to roll down my face. I don't know what got into me. I was completely overwhelmed, and couldn't begin to explain it. A weird and wonderful feeling came over me in a way that mere words cannot describe. I was standing there with my face in my hands, when Courtney tucked a tissue between my fingers. She wrapped her arm around my shoulder. When I glanced up to thank her, I could see that she too was crying.

It wasn't long before I found myself standing at the altar with hundreds of other people also seeking a solution to their troubled circumstances. I don't know how my feet found the courage to walk down to the front, but I felt a tugging on my heart that compelled me to take the first step. Crying, kneeling, bowing down at the altar, I was asking Jesus to forgive me and save me from the mess I had made of my life.

I asked Him to heal my broken heart and wounded soul. I needed Him to help me to get over the bitterness I still harbored over the past. I very much wanted to be happy and whole again. I told Jesus that if He were real, then He could do for me what He had done for Courtney, Melvin, Claudia and my mother. I wanted to feel and experience the love of God in the same way that they had so passionately described.

At the end of the service, some ushers escorted us through a door toward the back of the platform and explained what we had all had just experienced. They told us that we had answered the call to accept Jesus Christ as our personal Savior and that upon doing so, we would become born-again. This meant that our heart, mind and spirit would be renewed to the knowledge and understanding of Jesus Christ. They then led us in what was referred to as the "sinners' prayer". We all prayed in unison.

"Lord Jesus, I recognize that I am a sinner and that I need a Savior to save me from my sins. I believe that You died on the cross to redeem me from the curse of sin, and today I confess with my mouth and believe in my heart that God raised You from the dead. Come into my heart and abide; I choose

You to be the Lord of my life, now and forevermore. In Jesus' name I pray, amen."

After this, people were still crying and hugging one another; teens, grown men and women alike. The counselors congratulated us, handed out books and other reading materials and lovingly sent us on our way.

By the time I went outside, Courtney was eagerly waiting for me, again with open arms. She was so excited! During the ride home she also congratulated me on the awesome decision I had just made. She said that I was now a new creature in Christ and my life would never be the same again. To tell the truth, it did feel like some change had occurred, and though I still felt like plain old Sabrina, I was very anxious and excited to see where this new road of salvation would lead.

☽☾ • ☽☾ • ☽☾ ☽☾ • ☽☾ •

In the weeks and months that followed my conversion, I began to develop in both my relationship with Jesus, and with my swelling belly. Almost five months pregnant, I looked as though I would give birth at any moment. I was huge!

For the first time in years, I felt complete. So much had changed, in so many areas of my life, in such a short period of time. The irony in this whole thing is that I managed to turn myself into Courtney. Like she had when she first became a believer, I also went to church almost every day in the week. Sunday morning and evening services,

Monday prayer meetings, Wednesday Bible studies, and Friday night Young Adult's fellowship.

Not only was church services an integral part of my life, I even volunteered one Saturday a month at the church's soup kitchen, where we serve hot meals and distribute clothing to the poor and homeless. I can't help but laugh when I think about how the tables have turned on me. I really think God does have a sense of humor.

I was so hungry for God and had an insatiable desire to learn as much as I could about Him. I could not get enough of studying and knowing more about His Word. Since Earth Changers Church had their own bookstore on site, I was constantly buying new books, CDs and sermon tapes. If I don't already own every book my pastor has written, I'm almost there.

Bible study was by far my favorite class and despite my regular nausea and fatigue spells, I never missed a session. Pastor Dinero was a great teacher, and he really made the Bible make literal sense in today's day. He taught a lot about the principles of faith and love, and how to apply them in our daily lives. I could hardly believe the wealth of knowledge I gleaned in these few short months. My only regret was that it had taken me so long to recognize and yield to the unconditional love that God had for me.

I now understood why Courtney, Melvin, Claudia and now Gina were so enamored. It wasn't just hype. Jesus is the real deal, and unless you give Him a chance to prove

Himself in your life, you'll never know. That's what I learned in the past three months.

God had done wonderful things in my relationship with Gina. Since Grandie's passing, Miss Maxine was no longer obligated to stay with us. We tried to persuade her to stay, but she had another assignment, and moved out a week after the funeral. The babies and I have certainly missed her cooking.

So now it was just my mother and me alone in that big house. The day I gave my life to the Lord, I realized that things between us had to change. At first I didn't know how to address it, but God saw my heart and made a way. A few days after Miss Maxine left, I came home from Courtney's house to find Gina cooking dinner. I was never really a supporter of my mother's cooking, but she said that Miss Maxine had taught her a few things. I walked into the kitchen and sat at the table.

"Smells good," I complimented her. "What are you making?"

"Thank you. It's brown-stewed chicken with rice and steamed vegetables," she beamed proudly.

"Okay, don't hurt 'em, Ma!" She laughed at that. "Can I talk to you while you cook?"

"Sure, Bri. I can turn off the stove now if you want. It won't be a problem."

"No, no, no. You can continue. I just wanted to let you know what's been going on with me."

The look on her face was priceless, like she finally got the breakthrough she had been praying for. "All right, I'm listening."

"I'm pretty sure you've noticed by now, but Eric and I are over. We're not getting married and... I'm pregnant with twins." I stopped for her reaction.

"Oh, my God, Sabrina." She walked over to the chair I sat on and knelt down to hug me. "I figured you guys were going through something when I didn't see him come for Mom's funeral, but I didn't realize that the wedding was off. Are you all right? Is it because you're pregnant?"

"No. It's because he cheated on me with Monique and got her pregnant."

"Heavenly Father, what is this world coming to!" she shrieked, throwing her hands in the air.

I don't know why, but when she said that, I just burst out laughing hysterically. She looked at me as though I had gone mad, and little by little she started laughing uncontrollably too. We were rolling and had tears in our eyes, with absolutely no idea why.

When we were finally able to control ourselves, she held my hand tenderly and said, "God has given us a second chance, Sabrina. These children are a blessing and will bring so much joy and happiness to this house. Don't fret about a thing. I promise I'll be here for you now, whenever you need me. Okay?"

I mouthed okay back to her, and she hugged me again.

"So, you have officially moved back to Georgia, right?" she asked, as she returned to the stove.

"I'm not sure. I'm still trying to figure out what I ought to do."

"Well, pray about it, and I'll do the same. I know God will show you."

Chapter 17

Christmas and New Year's Day came and went. This was the first time since I was a child that the Holidays truly meant something. My mother and I had Christmas dinner with Courtney's parents, and we laughed and talked about how good God was to us all. Victor Wallace, Courtney's dad, pointed out that in spite of the hardships each of us had endured, we all still had so much to be thankful for.

"Who would have thought, a year ago, we all would end up where we are now? Courtney and Sabrina are friends again; Regina is a new woman with a lot to be proud of, and God has given my wife and me a second chance at love. I love you, Clarice. Merry Christmas, everybody!" he cheered.

"Merry Christmas!" we sang back in unison.

Mr. Wallace was absolutely right, because moving back to Georgia was the farthest thing from my mind even six months ago, let alone a year ago. Yet there I was, having Christmas dinner with my mother and old friends, and spending New Year's Eve in church. In the words of Sophia from *The Color Purple*, "I know'd dere is a God."

Now that I'm here, my life couldn't be any better. The emotional and spiritual healing I sought has also come to pass in my life. I still miss Melvin- I believe I always will- but I no longer grieve for him as much as before and am learning to let him go.

I have also discovered the peace in forgiveness. My mother and I grow closer daily, and we even pray together once in a while. She is so excited about becoming a grandmother and demonstrates her support to me in so many loving ways. She cooks, cleans and shops for the babies and accompanies me to the free clinic for my monthly check-ups.

There's still a part of me that doubts the truthfulness of the story she told about Grandie and Pete. But at this point, I have conceded that the truth will eventually come out in time. That is one of my prayers.

Joy and Peace have also become special friends of mine, and though trying days come, still, I rise. With all the activities I'm involved in, there is no time to weep and pine for Eric. I have not called or heard from him, and I'm okay with that. In light of all they have put me through, I have also learned to forgive him and Monique for their cruel deception, and actually wish them both the best.

Maybe this was the dawn that Grandie promised would come. Well, as usual, she was right.

☽☾ • ☽☾ • ☽☾ ☽☾ • ☽☾ •

A few days after New Year's, I finally found closure to the mystery of Gina's account of my so-called father. It had suddenly occurred to me that I had never opened the metal box Mel had given to Courtney for safekeeping. The day that she had given it to me, I had thrown it in the back of my car and had intended to go through it that night. Because of all the funeral planning and life changes I had experienced, I had simply forgotten about it.

Late one Saturday afternoon in my grandmother's bed, I sat reading a copy of the book, *Following God's Plan for Your Life*. It was a Christmas gift from Courtney. Something I read reminded me of the box and prompted me to run out and rummage through my car to find it. It was wedged in, hidden under the passenger seat and when I pulled it out, I frantically rushed back to my room to explore what was inside.

To my great surprise I found Grandie's will, the deed to her house, an In-Trust-For savings account, mutual fund documents naming Melvin and me as beneficiaries, and a stack of old savings and treasury bonds dating back from 1977. The face value was well over fifty thousand dollars!

Shortly after the funeral my mother had searched Grandie's room inside and out, looking for the deed to the house, but she never found it. My babies must have felt the absolute bliss that flooded my body, because they started to jump around and kick up a storm in my belly.

There was also a letter in a sealed envelope addressed to Peter Randolph. My heart skipped a beat as I recognized the name of Grandie's deceased husband. Using a nearby pen to break open the fold, I removed the four-page hand written letter, dated October 19, 1967 and read it.

Line by line, Grandie made her confession about killing her husband, her reasons and lack of regret for executing the act. However, she didn't give the details as to the method she had used, but it was enough to corroborate what Gina had disclosed to me.

Peter Randolph was indeed our father. Even though he was a dreadful man, it troubled me just a little that I never got the chance to know him. I wondered what his life had been like and what would have made him do such terrible things. Did he make it to heaven? Or did Grandie take that opportunity away from him? It disturbed me all over again, now that the truth was revealed.

I tried not to judge her; that was God's job. But it was still difficult to conceive that the gentle, mild grandmother I knew and cherished was capable of murder. I guess we never know what we are capable of doing until we are pushed to the limit. I hope it's safe to assume that that was the case with Grandie.

The following Monday morning I was at my grandmother's bank before they opened. I sat in my car and eagerly waited for the doors to open to the public.

Louis Muchado was the branch manager who assisted me. We sat in his office while he did the calculations and recalculations of the current value of the bonds, in addition to the balances of all her accounts, plus interest. With the exception of the current market value on the house, all other assets and accounts came to a whopping four hundred eighty-seven thousand, five hundred and nineteen dollars, and sixty-seven cents. That is $487,519.67, and it all now belonged to me. My money!

I did all I could to prevent myself from screaming wildly in Mr. Muchado's office.

"Could you repeat that, please?" I finally managed to ask.

"Four hundred and eighty seven-thousand, five hundred and nineteen dollars, and sixty-seven cents," he said again.

I got out of my chair and walked over to the window in his office and stared blankly into space. I don't know why, but I couldn't sit any longer. I tried to hold back the tears, but failed.

"Are you okay, Miss Richards?" Mr. Muchado asked tenderly.

"Yes, I'm fine. I'm just really surprised right now. I wasn't expecting this, you know." He looked as though he understood. "It is a large sum of money. What would you like to do with the funds?"

"Well, what are my options?" I asked, walking back to my seat. I removed two ply of tissue from a Kleenex box on the banker's desk to wipe my face.

"The bank offers several options. First, we could open a checking and savings account in your own name. Then you could meet with our investment representative at your convenience. He can offer you services and information we provide concerning mutual funds, IRAs and other high-to-moderate and moderate-to-low investment risks... I see that you are expecting a baby, and he could give you some information on setting up a college plan for your child. It's never too early to start you know." He chuckled.

"Two."

"Pardon me?"

"I'm expecting twins!" I beamed, as I corrected his misdiagnosis.

"Oh, that is exciting, Miss Richards. Congratulations are in order. Well, all the more reason for you to get these things in place as soon as possible. Did any option sound like it fits your needs?" he cleverly segued, getting back to the discussion about the money.

"Are those my only options?"

He was a bit reluctant to answer. "Or... we could just cut you a check for the whole amount."

"Tell you what I'll do. Please wire the entire amount to my personal bank account, and when I get my thoughts and plans together, I'll give you a call. How does that sound?"

"Very good, Miss Richards. That sounds very good. Let me say again how sorry I am for your loss. Your grandmother was a wonderful woman, and we loved her here at the bank. I truly mean that."

"Thank you, Mr. Muchado. I really appreciate that."

"Call me, Louis." He stood, handed me his card and shook my hand.

"Okay, Louis. Take care, and God bless you."

"Thank you and the same to you."

I walked out of the bank feeling like *four hundred thousand* more pounds had been loaded on me, but it felt fine. I jumped in my car and just sat there, completely awestruck, and then began praising God for His blessing, thanking Him for everything He had done for me.

Minutes after the initial shock wore off, I began to scream, stomp and flail my hands like Julia Roberts did in the movie *Pretty Woman*, in the scene where she squeals madly after casually accepting Richard Gere's four-thousand-dollar proposal. But this was four hundred thousand dollars!

Four hundred thousand dollars. I have four hundred thousand dollars? The more I said it the more outlandish it sounded. Yet, it was true.

Sadness reared its ugly head for a moment as I thought about Melvin. Half of this money had belonged to him, but since he was dead, it advanced to me as sole beneficiary. Then I thought of my mother.

I was sure she wasn't aware of Grandie's financial affairs, and the only thing she was entitled to was the house. Grandie had put her name on the deed and title at the time it was purchased and never removed it. At one point, she had made Gina a primary beneficiary on her personal accounts, but changed that when my mother's drug habit got way out of control.

Grandie was not about to let her drug addicted daughter squander and consume her life savings on crack cocaine and cheap liquor. She had been wise to make that decision. But now that my mother was completely changed; maybe she should have Mel's share. I believe it's what he would have wanted.

Then it came to me, almost like Melvin himself had just confirmed it in my spirit. His half should be shared evenly between Gina and Courtney. Right then I called Courtney, and she agreed to meet me for lunch.

☽☾ • ☽☾ • ☽☾ ☽☾ • ☽☾ •

"If you could name one thing that you want right now, what would it be?" I asked Courtney as we sat for lunch at Juno's Bar and Grill.

She laughed out loud. "What? Why do you ask?"

"No. You cannot answer a question with a question. This is not Jeopardy. Let's try this again. If you could name one thing in this whole world that you want right now, what would it be?"

"Okay. Well, besides the obvious new car, I could really use a vacation."

"Okay. That's good. Where would you want to go?"

"Um…I don't know, Hawaii? No, wait. Africa, or anywhere in the Caribbean."

"Courtney, you have to name one place," I pestered her.

"All right, um…Jamaica."

"Good choice. Done!"

"What! What are you talking about?" She looked puzzled.

I removed the financial papers from my bag and showed them to her. Courtney's eyes got so big as she read the documents line by line, and then she burst out in screams of elation. I couldn't help but join in. For a moment, we reverted back to the two silly schoolgirls who used to win money by "reading" people's minds.

"Shh! Keep it down!"

"What's the matter with you two?"

"Morons!"

Several patrons in the restaurant were chiding us, and to be perfectly honest, we couldn't care less.

"Is this for real!" Courtney exclaimed, covering her mouth with her hands to stifle her uncontainable squeals.

"Yes, Courtney, it's for real. And about one hundred and twenty thousand of it is yours. Melvin told me that he wanted you to have half of his share."

She pursed her lips and lifted her hands up to cover her eyes.

"Are you okay?" I asked her, trying not to cry myself.

She nodded as she picked up a napkin to wipe her face. She reached for my hand and we held on to each other for a few minutes without saying another word.

"So, Jamaica it is!" I said finally, breaking the emotive moment.

Courtney echoed, "Jamaica it is!"

Chapter 18

Needless to say, Gina was just as excited about the news of the money as Courtney and I had been. She said she was clueless about Grandie's accounts and admitted how grateful she was that she had been kept in the dark.

At one point in her past life, Gina would have stopped at nothing to do what was necessary to get her next high.

"Thank you, Jesus. Those days are over for me!" she confidently declared.

When she had finished jumping around for joy, she sat next to me on the couch and placed my head in her lap. My mother began to share the dreams and desires she had in her heart with me. It was something she had been praying about. As she combed through my hair, she told me that she wanted to use her portion of the money to start a new foundation for women on drugs.

The facility would be a residential shelter for battered, abused and broken women who had lost their zeal for life, but still hungered for someone to love and believe in them again. She wanted it to be a haven for them t receive the love of Jesus through people who genuine loved and cared for them. It would be a ministry similar to Teen-Challenge, but for women only. The name of the shelter would be called, **The Pamela Richards Haven of Hope,** in honor of Grandie. Of course I thought it was a splendid idea.

Gina talked about how it was for her when she was an addict. She explained that what she needed at the time, rather than to judge and condemn her, was someone to love and encourage her.

"I knew I wasn't doing the right thing, but I was hooked and I couldn't help myself or anybody else. Crack knew my name. It was always calling me. I was convinced that I couldn't live without drugs. If I didn't get high, I didn't feel normal. I was totally unable to function mentally, physically or emotionally without crack, and that's why I needed more and more of it. I knew the addiction could wind up killing me, but I didn't care. I hate to admit it, but I really had no regard for my own life, or anyone else's for that matter. It was either quit or die, and it's sad to say, but I would rather have died.

"When we couldn't steal from your grandmother anymore, Doomes started pimping me. I hated the idea at first, but it didn't take long for me to get used to it. With the money we made from prostituting, we were hardly ever without drugs. And even though it was my body that was used to get the money, Calvin was the one who kept the cash and rationed it as he pleased. Sabrina, it was hell living like that, and I'm so glad Jesus delivered and saved me from that lifestyle. I'm *so* glad."

My mother started to cry. I rose up and held onto her as she sobbed in my arms. She gently pulled away and continued talking.

"Sabrina, I have to tell you about the night your brother was killed. I was at my lowest point that night, and I wanted to end my life. That night I used some money I had hidden from Calvin to rent a motel room. I told him I wanted to do something romantic for him. He was surprised, but he bought the lie. I knew he had all the supply on him, and my plan was to wait until he fell asleep and steal it. I was going to go into Fairfield Park and smoke every bit of it until I overdosed and died. Why wait? It was the very thing that would kill me anyway, and I couldn't go on living in the debase condition that I was in. While Calvin slept, I managed to get the stash and some money from his jacket pocket and as I made my way to the door, your brother called me on the phone he had bought for me a few weeks earlier."

I recalled being upset at Melvin about getting Gina a phone, because I figured that she would turn around and sell it. But I didn't tell her that. "I remember when he bought that for you. He told me he wanted to check up on you periodically, to make sure you were all right," was all I said.

"Yes, and he called at the wrong time. Well, I take that back, because after all is said and done, I can now say it was the right time. But at that moment it wasn't good for me. The ringer was so loud, and it seemed like it was amplified even louder than usual at that particular moment. I fumbled to answer it before the noise woke up Calvin, but it was too late. He got up and saw that I was fully dressed with shoes on, obviously on my way out, and he knew I was up to something. I tried to act normal by speaking casually to Melvin. He asked me where I was and without thinking I told him. I asked him where he was, and he said he had come home from school for the weekend. Calvin started barking at me, 'Where the hell do you think you're going?' Sabrina, I tell you I was so scared I could hardly think.

"Melvin was asking me all sorts of questions, but I was not listening or responding to him. All that was on my mind was, how in the world am I going to get out of this one? Calvin got up to check his pockets, and that's when all hell broke loose in that motel. He jumped across the room and smacked me in the face so hard, that the phone went flying and cracked against the wall. He took a gun from his bag and beat me mercilessly with the butt. I felt like I was going to die at any moment. I can't recall the exact time frame, but it seemed like hours had passed. All I know is that at some point Melvin came bolting through the door. I remember unlocking it hours earlier so that I could slip out with ease."

"Wait a minute, I thought you *asked* Mel to come and get you from the motel?" I interjected.

"Yeah, that's what I told the cops. But I would never do that. Even in all my mess, I wouldn't deliberately put either of you in harm's way like that. I lied to the cops because I didn't want anyone to know that I had contemplated suicide. When Calvin had the gun to my head, I realized that I wasn't ready to die. I silently vowed to God that if He helped me just one more time, I would turn my life over to Him. That's exactly when Melvin rushed Calvin and, well, you know the rest."

I sat there stunned as I listened to what it was like for my mother during her years of addiction. What was even more staggering was hearing what really led my brother to the motel where he was shot. I wondered if he knew that that was the way everything would end up. Did he pray before going over there? What did God tell him? I will only know the answers when I see him again in heaven.

I had spent so many years being angry with Gina, that I had no idea of the struggles she had faced. I didn't know about the prostitution, or the suicidal thoughts. God had really brought her from a mighty long place, and I was truly thankful for the woman she had become.

What a great pleasure to see her so full of vision and zest for the future. She was as happy as she had ever been, and was determined to dedicate the rest of her life to serving God and helping women who are still living in the hopelessness with which she once struggled. And for the first time, I was starting to understand the sacrifice Melvin made; his earthly life for her eternal life. Melvin was truly a co-laborer with Christ. I could only hope one day to be worthy of such a privilege.

"Mom, I'm glad that you're here, and I'm sorry that I wasn't more compassionate toward you when you needed help. Please forgive me." I needed to say those words to her. It was about time.

"Oh, Sabrina, my beautiful daughter. I'm the one that needs your forgiveness. I love you and I'm so thankful for what God has done for us."

I sat up all the way and looked her in the eyes. "Mommy, I forgive you. I'm ready to bury the pain of the past and look ahead to the bright tomorrow that God has in store for us."

She took my hand in hers and replied softly, "Me too, Sabrina. Me, too."

☾ • ☾ • ☾ ☾ • ☾ •

Three weeks after my first meeting with Mr. Muchado, I took him up on the offer to meet with the bank's investment representative, Jonmark Cash. With a name like that, I felt pretty confident that he would know where to put my cash. The options were endless, but I was only interested in safely nesting the funds for a long period of time. I was never the gambling kind, so stock marketing and other high-risk ventures were of no interest to me.

After an hour of weighing the options, we finally concluded that life insurance, savings bonds and mutual funds were the best way to go. With no social security numbers yet available, my unborn children could not yet be made beneficiaries. But since I planned to make Courtney their godmother, I made her primary and my mother secondary. In all, I diversified about one hundred and eighty-thousand dollars and kept the remaining liquid balance in a personal, interest-bearing checking and savings account.

Outstanding and way overdue were the numerous bills I left back in New York. Creditors from everywhere were sure to be beating down my door by now, but thanks to God and Grandie, every one of them would soon be stamped: PAID IN FULL!

Single motherhood would not find me deep in debt. What a rare but incredible relief that was. Having money, and lots of it, definitely had its perks. The week of Courtney's school spring recess, we went to a day spa to pamper ourselves with full body massages, facial treatments and manicures and pedicures. That same day we had a sleepover in one of Atlanta's most luxurious hotels, the chain where guests of the Oprah Winfrey Show stayed. We also shopped till we dropped. I mean, literally dropped.

Walking out of Neiman Marcus one afternoon, Courtney took the lead. We were carrying so many bags that they blocked the view of a few carpeted steps leading to the other side of the mall. As she tripped down the first, second and finally the third step, I, with my big belly and all, toppled right over her, landing on my rear end. Several people standing around came to our assistance, but by that time we were laughing hysterically. The babies were fine. No major damage was done except maybe to my new Gucci shades that I had crushed in the process. Luckily for me, Neiman Marcus exchanged them for a brand new pair at no extra cost.

We visited a few travel agents to book our trip to Jamaica, but they all said I was "too pregnant" to fly international. Courtney and I tried very hard to convince them that I was only six months, but they were not buying it.

All they would say was, "We understand. However, as a preventive measure, the airlines we do business with will require consent in the form of a doctor's note allowing you to fly."

The truth was that I didn't really have a specific doctor. In the last five months, all I did to maintain a relatively healthy pregnancy was visit the free health center for the monthly health checks and take the sample vitamins Dr. Val had kindly given to me.

Naturally, we were both disappointed and decided our trip to the Caribbean was the first thing we would take after the babies were born and old enough to sleep through the night. We might even bring them with us and hire a nanny. Like they say in Jamaica, 'no problem'. We have options now, don't we?

Speaking of options, now that I had the money and could afford to have the abortion, it was no longer an alternative for me. I promised God that I would stop pursuing my selfish plans to terminate the precious gifts He had blessed me with. While I could not see it before, He had always had a plan for us. The financial means were already provided, and I am confident that I will be married someday to the right man. All I have to do is trust God to work it out for me.

He revealed to me that abortion was wrong and no matter how hard I tried to justify myself, committing such an act is a sin. There is no right to choose. The gift of conception is a privilege not a right. I now understand that even though it is my body, God is the giver of life, and no one else but Him has the right or sovereignty to take it away. Even at their embryonic stage, my babies still had a soul and a spirit, and I would never have been able to find a good enough excuse to justify terminating their existence.

I couldn't help but think about Niqi's many terminated pregnancies and wondered if God would hold it against her. When I prayed for her, God showed me that forgiveness is granted for the sin of abortion, but only if we repent and ask for it. I also wondered if I'd ever get the chance to tell Niqi that.

As my pregnancy developed, I had grown to love my children very much and could hardly wait to meet them. Every kick and tumble felt so wonderful and I eagerly looked forward to June 19th, their expected due date.

Two and a half months to go, and their daddy was still in the dark about their existence.

The last time I had spoken to Eric, I had my phone number changed, and haven't spoken to him again since then. I really struggled with how to go about being open and honest with him. It was a combination of fear and shame that made it easier to keep him in the dark for so long. I just didn't know how Eric would react to my pregnancy. I was nervous that he might not take it well. I was also a little self-conscious to see him with this big ol' belly I heaved around with me.

As much as I loved being pregnant now, I really wanted to be striking, stunning and fabulous the next time I was seen in New York. Not thirty-six pounds overweight and counting. The shame I felt was strictly due to my initial consideration to abort. I knew that I would have to tell him that part of the story and was uncomfortable about it.

After much deliberation, I finally built up the courage to go to New York and face Eric. It was really in prayer that I realized I didn't need to be fearful about anything. I would not allow my heart to be troubled about this whole "Eric" situation. I didn't do anything wrong, and he had every right to know the truth. Only then would I truly be made free.

I told my mother and Courtney about my decision and they agreed it was the right thing to do. Courtney offered to accompany me to the Big Apple, but I insisted it was something I needed to do alone. She understood perfectly.

Chapter 19

JFK International Airport was unusually quiet and empty for a weekend day. Two-thirty on a Saturday afternoon and I could count all the people in the gating area waiting to board their flight. As soon as passengers were allowed to disembark, I headed straight for the food court and parked my new Dooney and Bourke luggage under the countertop at Sbarro's pizzeria.

Those awful-tasting blue potato chips the airline had served were just not doing it, even though I ate three bags. They were gross but it was all they had. To make up for it, I thoughtfully treated my babies to a platter of Chicken Parmesan with Baked Ziti, a plain slice of pizza and a bottle of apple juice, and three chocolate chip cookies for myself.

After feeding time was over, I descended to the passenger pick-up area to hail a cab. It was a relatively chilly 58-degree April afternoon, and I was glad that I had worn my new wool Poncho. Wet pavements and slick sidewalks were the leftover evidence that it had rained earlier.

I joined the long line at the taxi stand, but after only a minute or so, a kind man closer to the front offered me his place in line. Soon after, a classy black Lincoln Town Car pulled up to the curb. The driver, a tall, handsome white man dressed in a black suit and red tie got out of the car to put my luggage in the trunk. One thing's for sure, the pregnancy factor did have its perks.

"Good day ma'am. Where to?" he asked, when we were both in the car.

"The Crowne Plaza Hotel." The driver nodded his head and pulled away.

Before I left Georgia, I spoke with Claudia and she offered to pick me up from JFK upon my arrival. She even insisted that I stay with her and Silvia. I had all the best intentions to spend time with them, but I needed a couple days alone to sort things out with Eric. The girls were so anxious to see me with my bulging belly, and I was just as eager to see them.

Claudia said that Silvia was doing very well adjusting to life in New York. She had found a job working behind the scenes at a television talk show, and made pretty good money as a make-up artist for the guests of the show.

The relationship they once had would never be the same, but Claudia said the new one they were building would go beyond the old, especially since they built it on forgiveness and on Christ. They even went to church together on a regular basis. I was so happy for them.

One of the best lessons I learned about God was that He is a God of restoration, especially in terms of relationships. It's really quite amazing how He does it, and in the end, only He can get the glory.

I've come to the conclusion that as human beings, we have the propensity to be a naturally destructive species, particularly when it comes to relating to other people. When left up to us, we somehow manage to manipulate, tear down and mistreat the very people we ought to love and cherish the most.

Without God at the center, these damaged relationships usually remain severed without any chance for repair. However, when we come to our senses and choose to invite God in, the results are always miraculous.

From a distance, God is able to precisely decipher who, what, when and why certain quandaries or difficulties arise in a relationship. He can pinpoint root causes that the people involved are completely blind to. God is then able to sort through the lunacy, rubbish and confusion. He separates the wheat from the chaff; the good seed from the bad seeds, leaving only what is vital and desirable. With the garbage out of the way, we are then able to work through and forgive, and find the healing necessary to mend broken relationships. When God steps in to turn the circumstance around, you have no choice but to admit that, "God did it!"

I marvel when I take note; Claudia and Silvia, Courtney and me, and even my mother and me. We all found the way to forgiveness. Never once did I imagine that my mother and I could ever come to terms with past hurts and resolve our issues. Little by little we've been working it out, but as Claudia had said, things would never be as they once were, but we would aim to make them better.

Not too long ago there were severe chinks in the chain that once connected each ruined relationship, but when God got involved, He amazingly put the links back together. Before I met Jesus Christ, I thought that was an impossible feat. I now know that what is impossible for us is always possible with God. Another lesson learned.

I sometimes wondered what God would do, if anything, to restore the relationship between Eric and me. Was there even hope at this stage? I didn't even know how I felt about him anymore. I mean, I've forgiven him, and there is no more bitterness. I just can't tell if I am still romantically attached to him anymore. It was only five months since the last time we had talked and I know there were no tender loving feelings then. Meeting him face to face may be the only way to tell.

꒰꒱ • ꒰꒱ • ꒰꒱ ꒰꒱ • ꒰꒱ •

At four hundred and thirty-seven dollars each night, the Crowne Plaza Hotel was no different from the hundred dollar-a-night hotels I had stayed in before. My room was on the 19th floor and had a great view of Times Square, but I could have stayed at the Double Tree and paid way less for the same scenery. Nevertheless, for the next couple of days, the Plaza was my home and I was determined to make the best of it.

I looked forward to seeing all the lights from the buildings that would illuminate the city and the Manhattan skyline once nightfall came. It was only four thirty, and I was exhausted. All that traveling wore me out and I needed a nap. But before that, I called Eric and arranged to meet for dinner.

☾☾ • ☾☾ • ☾☾ ☾☾ • ☾☾ •

Ten minutes after nine. Eric was late. We were supposed to meet at the Bubba Gump Shrimp Restaurant at eight-thirty, and he said he would probably be there before me. Since my hotel was only three blocks away, I knew that wasn't very likely. Even so, I had jumped into a cab for the short ride; the meter didn't even budge from my entrance to my exit. It's just that walking, or waddling rather, for more than five minutes at a time was such a challenge for me. It would more than likely have taken me close to an hour to get to my six-minutes-away destination.

I had been so nervous when I made the call to Eric. He was very surprised to hear my voice on the other end of the line and even more surprised when he heard I was in town. He was at his parents' house and wanted to play catch-up.

"How have you been?" "Where have you been?" "Why did you change your number?" "What's your new number?"

I promised we would talk about everything once we met, and he said it would only take him an hour to get dressed.

Eric had agreed to be at the restaurant at eight-thirty or earlier and, looking at the time now, I wondered if he would come at all. Could it be that his other baby momma held him up? *Hmm.* This momma, however, was getting very hungry, so I went ahead and ordered without him.

"Couldn't wait for me, huh?" said a familiar voice.

Without looking up, I shook my head, pointed to my watch, and proceeded to stuff a forkful of Teriyaki shrimp into my mouth.

"You're late, and I couldn't wait." I explained without apology.

With a mouthful, I looked up to see my ex standing next to my table. Surprisingly, my heart didn't go pitter-patter, but he did look good, as always.

He kissed me on the cheek, brought out a bouquet of roses from behind his back, and sat on the other end of the booth. He smelled as good as he looked. *Hmm, Curve, of course.*

"I'm sorry. There was an accident on the FDR and traffic was backed up to 125th Street. These are for you," he said, handing me the flowers. I was beginning to think that Eric liked plant life more than I did.

"Thank you, they're beautiful," I replied politely.

"No, you're beautiful. Sabrina, I really mean it. Wow, you look radiant."

He wasn't lying. I had picked out this fabulous Jean Paul Gaultier dress that looked perfect over my belly. And it wasn't even a maternity dress. I couldn't afford to let him see me looking like a heifer. I'm *so* glad that he noticed.

"Why, thank you." I replied casually. "Are you going to order?"

"Um, yeah, sure. I'm just a little shocked you chose this place, because I know you don't like shrimp at all."

"Yeah, I know." I took a sip of my lemonade.

He was right. I didn't like shrimp, but apparently the babies did. It was one of the many cravings that plagued my pregnancy. I was so nervous about telling him. I didn't know where to start. I waited for the perfect opening.

Troy, the waiter, stopped at our table to take Eric's order. As he handed over the menu back to Troy, Eric spoke in a low voice.

"Bri, I really want you to know just how sorry I am about how things fell apart between us. You may not believe me, but I never wanted to hurt you. I guess I was just scared about the whole marriage thing, and just lost it... I got carried away in the heat of the moment."

He took my hand in his, as he often did when making an apology, and looked into my eyes. I should have interrupted him, but allowed him to finish instead.

"Hurting you was the worst mistake of my entire life, and I'm sorry." He stopped.

That's it? I thought to myself. What, no begging and pleading for me to take him back? No big declaration of his undying love for me... Well, I guess it was now my turn.

"Look, Eric…"

"Wait, I'm not done."

"Oh, I'm sorry. Go ahead." I insisted.

"It's no secret anymore that Monique was pregnant and that I am the father. Well, she had the baby almost a month ago, a little boy. His name is Gavin."

Eric began to choke up. At first I thought it was from the overwhelming joy of being a proud daddy, but as he continued, it became clear that something else was wrong.

"Are you all right?" I asked, genuinely concerned. He ignored my question and continued his speech.

"Gavin was born prematurely with cerebral palsy, and he's blind."

There was silence at our table. What the heck does one say after something like that? It seemed like an eternity before either of us said another word. The sound of the plate smacking the table broke the hush and I looked up to thank Troy, more for breaking the silence than for bringing the food. I stammered a bit before finally getting the words to come out straight.

"Eric, I'm so sorry...I feel like such an idiot. I don't know what to say."

It was the truth.

"You don't have to say anything, Sabrina. You know what they say, what goes around comes back around again. It's karma, you know."

"No, I don't believe that. I'm not going to lie to you, Eric. I was one devastated woman when I found out about you and Monique, but in the past few months I've learned that God gives us second chances, no matter how badly we mess up; even if we don't deserve it. Now I don't know why Gavin was born the way he was, but he is still your son, and a blessing. And to prove that God is a God of second chances, well, just look..."

Here it came; this was my segue, the opening I was waiting for.

I stood up and bared my belly. Eric's jaw hit the table and for more than thirty seconds his face stayed frozen in that position. His face contorted from a look of shock, to a frown, then finally to a look of blatant disbelief.

"Twins," was all I could say, shrugging my shoulders and biting my bottom lip.

"Is that what you meant when you said you would 'get rid of these babies'?" Eric finally spoke.

"Yes. But I've had a change of heart since then, and I'm really sorry that I didn't tell you earlier."

I wiggled back into the booth and explained my side of the story to him... every detail from the last time we saw each other in the hospital, to the re-established relationships with my mother and Courtney, to my new relationship with God and the Earth Changers Church. It took him a while to absorb it all, but after a three-hour long discussion, he seemed to be at peace with everything.

"So; how far along are you? Do you know what we're having?" he inquired.

"I'll be seven months next week, and no, I want to be surprised. It'll probably be like Mel and me, or Erica and you."

"Whoa! We're having twin babies, Sabrina? Oh, man, I..." He was at a complete loss for words.

"I know it's a big deal, Eric, and I just sprang it on you out of the clear blue sky. I was in shock too when I first found out. But we're here now, and I need to know that you'll be there for your children. You have three children now, and you'll need to be there for all of them."

"Of course, I'll be there. You know that."

I gave him a look that clearly said, *No, I don't!* But I only responded by saying, "Eric, I hear what you're saying, but I guess we'll just have to wait and see."

"I know. My track record is bad and you have every reason to hate me for what I did to you. I'm really sorry, Sabrina."

He looked genuinely forlorn. I took his hand, smiled at him, and assured him that I had forgiven and let go of everything that had happened. The past was the past, and I wanted to leave it that way. In turn, I also asked his forgiveness for my keeping the truth about his children from him for so long. Without a second thought, he happily granted it.

At half past eleven, Eric had hardly touched his meal. I beckoned for the waiter, and asked him to wrap up the food and give us the check. Excusing myself from the table, I went to the ladies' room and on my way back, I stopped to pay the bill. Eric was slightly perturbed by that, but I insisted that it was my treat. Besides, I invited him out; it was only right that I pay.

As I stood to leave, he offered me a ride back to my hotel. I gladly accepted. I waited in front of the restaurant while he ran to the garage to get his car. In just about five minutes, as expected, we pulled up in front of the hotel. We sat there in complete silence until he worked up the nerve to speak.

"Are you tired? You probably are, right? With traveling all day and everything."

"Um, no, not really. I slept this afternoon." I admitted.

"You want to go for a drive?" he inquired.

"Where to at this hour of the night?"

"Come on, you'll see."

We exchanged only a few words during the drive and twenty minutes later he parked in a lot in City Island overlooking the water. The passengers in other cars, most with tinted windows, were kissing and engaging in a whole lot more.

Eric's house was only a five-minute drive away. In our old life, we used to come here to do the same thing. I started to feel uneasy, wondering what his intentions were, but when he got out to open my door, I was reassured. We were clearly not supposed to be here because there were several **NO PARKING AFTER DUSK** signs posted. Fortunately for the lovers, the rule wasn't strictly enforced.

Occasionally patrol officers would cruise by, but they were mostly looking for drugs and other criminal activities. We walked over to the benches close to the water's edge. It was a cool, beautiful spring evening. The stars were out and the water was full of boaters on their yachts, also stargazing and enjoying the moonlight.

"Are you comfortable?" Eric asked, interrupting my musing.

I only nodded.

"You're probably wondering why I brought you out here." He paused. When I didn't respond, he continued.

"I don't know myself. I just wanted us to talk some more." He shrugged his shoulders as if he was having trouble expressing himself.

"Okay," I said skeptically. "What do you want to talk about?"

"Anything... everything. Is there anything you want to ask me?"

Of course there was. There were still so many unanswered questions. I wanted to know what transpired between him and *her*, but I refused to bring up the subject.

"Is there anything you want to tell me?"

"Sabrina, I know you must have a ton of questions about what happened between Monique and me. Whatever you want to ask, I'm willing to be completely truthful and honest with you."

This was the opportunity I had waited months, many months for. I did want to know what had happened between him and Niqi. Why her? If he had doubts, why didn't he come to me? I had a million questions, but I wanted to be careful in how I asked them.

"Okay, Eric. Earlier in the restaurant, you said that you were scared about getting married. What were you so afraid of, and why didn't you just come to me. Why couldn't you just have been honest from the start?"

"All right. Sabrina, from the day I met you I knew you were the one for me. We used to have so much fun and did so many things together. But in the last year or so, you just changed so much. I know that it was really rough for you when your brother died, and all I wanted was to be there for you. It killed me to see you so upset and unhappy, but little by little you just kept pushing me away. I wanted to respect your space by giving you the time you needed, but you never let me in. It felt like you were pulling away and I didn't know how to handle it. Every time I would suggest we do something or talk, you would always say 'later'. You barely even let me touch you, and I felt neglected and rejected."

He sighed deeply, and then continued.

"When you went away to Georgia to see after your grandmother, Monique just made herself available. At first we just talked about you, and all that you were going through with losing Melvin, and your grandmother's failing health. I began to share with her how isolated I felt in our relationship. Looking back, I realize that I shouldn't have. But the truth is, she was the closest person to you, and I was just hoping that she could tell me something to help me understand how to handle the situation. One moment we were talking about you and me, and the next moment she and I wound up in a compromising situation. The whole thing just got way out of hand, and I didn't know how to stop it. By the time you came back to New York, things had already gone too far. But you have to believe me when I tell you that I never intended for things to end up the way they did. I swear to you."

He intently searched my face for a reaction and when I gave none, he kept on going.

"When Monique got pregnant, it felt like my whole world had come crashing down. I was caught in a web of confusion and deception and didn't know how to get out. I got scared and had no idea what to do."

"You could have told the truth. You should have said something to me."

"Do you think that would have made things easier? I contemplated every possible scenario, and nothing seemed like the best thing to do."

"No. What you mean is that, there was no easy way out, Eric. That's what you were looking for. I know that I was somewhat withdrawn, but I had no idea you felt the way you did. We were planning a life together. You should have done everything in your power to get me to listen. I didn't realize I made you feel so rejected. That was never my intention. I just needed more time to grieve."

"I knew that. I just wanted to grieve with you. When you left New York, I was so emotionally and physically bankrupt, but at the same time, I wanted to do the right thing by Monique. After all, I *was* the one who got her pregnant. That's what these past months have been all about. I felt guilty, and once again, didn't know what direction to take. But if ever you think for one minute that what Monique and I had was anything like what we had, then you're wrong. No other woman could ever take your place."

"Oh, really?" I interjected. "What about the pictures, Eric? I found pictures of you and her together and you didn't seem all that bored to me," I spat out at him, trying not to sound embittered.

"I know. I was caught up, Sabrina. I know that I could never say anything that will make you understand, but I just got caught up in the drama of it all. It was all a big illusion. After Gavin was born, I decided to break off all romantic ties with Monique. I felt that his illness was the consequence of what Monique and I did, and I couldn't continue being with her. She was angry and couldn't understand it, but I know it's the right thing to do. She thinks that I'm running away because the baby is challenged and that I want nothing to do with him. But nothing could be further from the truth. I love my son and will always be there for him, in every way a father should. I just can't continue to be with someone I don't love and stay just out of a sense of guilt. It's not fair to Gavin or Monique.

"I also know that what I did was not fair to you, and I can't apologize enough to you, Sabrina. I hurt you and I think I'll be sorry for the rest of my life. I don't know what else to say, but that's the whole truth."

As much as I had waited all this time to learn the truth, hearing it now brought up painful emotions I had tried so hard to erase. I felt the tears begin to sting my eyes, but I didn't hide them from him. I reached into my bag for a piece of tissue and dabbed the corners of my eyes.

"Well, Eric, you've said quite a lot and I thank you for your honesty. It really means a lot, and it helps to bring some closure. I needed that. I'm sorry that things didn't work out the way you expected it to, but you never know. Maybe you'll have better luck with love the next time around, huh?"

I can't explain why, but I began to feel really sorry for Monique. The pain of losing the man you love is one

I'm all too familiar with, and I understand more than anyone what she must be going through right now.

Eric did find more to say. He admitted that his parents are still livid about everything, and that Erica barely talks to him. They told him he'd better get on his hands and knees and beg God to forgive him and bring Sabrina back.

That sounded like his mother. He said that's what he recently started to do. He confessed that he never understood the meaning of "you don't know what you've got till it's gone," until he lost me. Then he went for the kill.

"So, what about you?"

"What about me?" I shot back. What did he expect me to say?

"You said earlier tonight, at the restaurant, that God is a God of second chances. What about you?"

Whoa! I wasn't expecting that one. I didn't even know how to answer. *Think quickly!*

"I'm not God." That was the best I could come up with. There was a pause, only about fifteen seconds, but it seemed a whole lot longer. I continued.

"Look, Eric, I'm not sure what you want me to say, okay, but I'm not the same old Sabrina who left New York six months ago. I'm a Christian woman now and totally committed to living a Christian lifestyle. You of all people know how I used to feel about the whole Christian thing. At one time, I couldn't wait to get away from Courtney, and I was completely uncomfortable when being around

Claudia for more than ten minutes. I didn't know God, and was resentful toward Him for taking Mel. But after everything that happened between you, Niqi, and me, I was completely lost. I was so hurt and overcome with heartache; there were even times when I felt like I didn't want to go on. You see, the problem was that I had built my foundation on sand. You were everything to me: mind, soul and body. I idolized you, and not God, and because you are merely a man, who also doesn't know God, it's only natural that you would fail me. I had exalted and esteemed you to a higher degree than the Most High.

"In these few short months, I've realized that when we misplace the importance of people and things in our lives, it turns into idolatry, and eventually it will fall apart. Building any relationship on that kind of foundation is like the foolish man who built his house on the sand. When the rains and the storm came, the foundation couldn't hold it together; it all came tumbling down. That's what happened to me, and do you know who was there to help put *me* back together again? It wasn't you, Eric.

"You were the cause, Jesus *is* the cure. Don't get me wrong, I'm not blaming you for everything. I was the one who had the wrong priorities in order. I didn't get it then, but I get it now. One thing I always want you to remember is: the key to lasting happiness is to seek God first and everything that pleases Him. Then, and only then, will your life fall correctly into place. And that's Bible! I need you to know that the changes I made in my life are real, and *if* you were to be in my future, you would have to make those changes too. So I can't stand here and tell you that we can pick up right where we left off, because we can't."

"Man, that's intense. You really have changed alot, Sabrina. You said a lot of really inspiring things, and lately I've been thinking about how I need to prioritize and get my own life in order. I even went to church with my parents a few weeks ago."

"That's good, Eric. God will show you how to do it, just like he showed me. He's not a respecter of people." *Oh my gosh, I sounded like my pastor.*

"Well, what if I said, yes."

"Yes, to what?"

"What if I committed myself to making those changes the same way you did? What then?"

"I don't know, Eric. I'd have to pray about that, and let God decide if that's the best thing for either of us."

"Okay, okay. That's good. Let's pray right now."

"What! No, you're crazy. This is not a joke!"

He looked at me, serious as a judge.

"Who's joking, Sabrina? I do not want to live another day without you. I can't. And I'll do whatever it takes to make that possible."

He got down on the dirty concrete with glass splinters, trash and gum scattered everywhere, clasped his hands in the prayer position and began to pray out loud.

"Dear God, I'm so sorry for the way that I hurt Sabrina. I was selfish and wicked, and I need you to forgive me. Sabrina says that you give second chances, and if you give me a second chance with her, I promise to spend the rest of my life making her happy. I also realize that I need to get right with you, but I need you to show me what to do. Please hear my prayer and bless my request, even though I don't deserve it. In your name, amen."

He stood back up, and brushed the debris off his pants.

"It's 'in Jesus' name'," I corrected him.

"Excuse me?"

"When you pray, you're supposed to ask for what you want in Jesus' name."

"Oh, okay, thanks." He knelt back down on the filthy pavement and concluded:

"God, I ask this prayer in Jesus' name, amen."

"You're insane," I told him. When he stood up again, I started walking back to the car.

"Where are you going?" He asked, following behind me.

"It's late, Eric. I'm tired now and I really need to use the bathroom. Please take me back to my hotel."

Since his house was a few minutes away, he suggested that I use his bathroom. I really didn't feel comfortable about going to his house. Something told me not to go, but I overrode the instinct. I didn't think I could hold out until we got back to Manhattan. I gave him a *-you bet-*

ter *not try anything with me-* look that spoke volumes. He swore he wouldn't dare cross that line. Not that I thought he would, but I just wanted to make myself perfectly clear.

)⌒ •)⌒ •)⌒)⌒ •)⌒ •

Immediately after Eric pushed the front door open and we stepped into his living room, unexpected drama unfolded. Niqi was sitting on the sofa in the living room, the baby in the infant seat next to her. As soon as she saw him, she plunged her fists into the couch to give herself a boost.

The girl had put on a lot of extra weight since the pregnancy, and she was not that small to begin with. She had to be at least twenty pounds over her normal size. I certainly did not expect to see her here, and by the look on Eric's face, it was obvious that he was also surprised by the unexpected visit. I don't know why, though, because evidently she had a key to his house, for crying out loud! She obviously had liberal access.

It quickly became apparent that I should not be here, and the fiery sting of regret suddenly began to gnaw at me. Since she hadn't seen me yet, I had a great mind to make an about-face and take a taxi back to my hotel. But I still had to use the bathroom. She marched toward Eric.

"Where have you been all night? I've been calling you. Gavin is..."

The sight of me stopped her in mid-sentence. Monique looked like the wind was knocked out of her when she saw my protruding belly. She fixed her eyes on her baby's father and with distress evident in her tone, asked him, "Eric, what the hell is going on?"

Before he could answer, I interjected. "Excuse me, I have to go to the powder room." I made my way down the hall to the bathroom.

Eric was trying to calm her down by telling her there was nothing going on. She asked about my pregnancy and whether he was the father. *What was she, stupid?* Eric kept telling her that there were things he needed to work out with me, and that everything would be all right.

"Did you leave me to be with her?" I heard Monique scream. "It's because Gavin isn't a normal child, isn't it? That's why you want to go back to her! Do you know that she's the reason our son was born this way?"

Then she started to grovel. "Eric, you still love *me*, right?"

There was such refuge in the bathroom. I wished I could have stayed forever. I really didn't want to go back out to the drama that was unfolding between Eric and Monique. If only I could still fit through the window. I shouldn't have come here, and had a bad feeling this was going to get ugly.

When he didn't answer her, Niqi started to cry. She was telling him that Gavin had had a cold and had come down with flu-like symptoms. She accused him of being unfair and selfish to their son. She complained that she had been calling him all evening, but instead of checking in on Gavin, Eric was out rendezvousing with "that goose". It was safe to assume that she was referring to me. Eric tried to get her to leave, promising that he would be at her place shortly with anything the baby needed.

Unless I had turned into an elephant within the last five minutes, it shouldn't have taken me this long to urinate. I'd already spent ten minutes in the bathroom. I took a deep breath and stepped out of my safe haven into the hostile environment.

"Eric, I'm fine. I'll just grab a cab. Okay?" I said, making a move for the door.

"Bri, wait. Give me a sec, all right. I'll take you. Just give me one minute," he pleaded.

"The hell you are!" Monique butted in. "You are not going anywhere Eric, and neither are you." She looked at me.

"Monique, I don't have anything to say to you. As far as I'm concerned you and I are over, and I don't owe you any explanation," I said.

"Not as far as *I'm* concerned. My son was born blind and mentally disabled, and it's all your fault. Look at him! You attacked and assaulted me when I told you I was pregnant, and now, because of you, I have a sick child who will never be normal, not one day of his life! So, no Sabrina, everything is *not* over between you and me."

Monique was livid. I couldn't say a word. Was it really my fault Gavin was born abnormal? I did get pretty rough with her the day we came to blows in my apartment.

This was too much, and I just wanted to be back in Georgia, or over at Claudia's, or anywhere but here.

"And now you're pregnant! Well, ain't this something. Is that how you plan to get Eric to come back to you?"

"That's enough, Monique!" Eric came to my defense when Gavin started to cry. "Don't do this in front of the baby."

I looked at Eric and put up my hand. "I'm out of here. This is for the birds and I'm no bird. So if you'll excuse me, I'm going back to my hotel."

I moved toward the door as fast as my belly would allow me, and instead of consoling her child, Monique came charging after me. Eric trotted behind, calling after her.

"Monique! Monique, get back in here!"

Just make it down the steps, I coached myself.

As I made my descent, holding securely onto the railing, I heard the madwoman behind me say, "Have a nice trip, skank!"

I lost my footing and tumbled down the remaining six steps, landing on my back, my head bumping into the concrete. Although my eyes were closed and my body motionless, I heard Eric shout, "Oh, my God! What the hell is wrong with you? You stupid…"

After that, I blacked out.

Chapter 20

Grandie's garden had never looked more beautiful. The flowerbeds bore lilies, violets, tulips and roses of every color in the rainbow. They stood erect; bathing in the bright sunlight that sustained their flourishing life.

My grandmother sat comfortably on her porch swing as Gina stood behind her, combing through her lovely silver tresses and massaging her scalp. There was an open container of Dax hair oil perched on the window ledge. Melvin stood by, watering the flower garden. They all were completely amused by Courtney and me as we challenged each other to a game of Jacks.

"You're out. It's my turn!" I contested Courtney's last move.

"No, I'm not. I picked up all six. Look!" She opened her hand to prove her point.

"Yeah, but your finger touched that one. Look, it moved. It's my turn now. You're out."

The two of us went back and forth disputing the charge I had placed against her move. Neither of us was willing to yield.

"Fine! I'm not playing with you anymore." I hopped up from the bottom of the porch stairs, pouting. With arms folded, I marched heatedly up one, two, three steps. I didn't see it coming, but right then Mel mischievously turned the hose on me to cool me down. By the time my foot hit the fourth step, the force of the cold water startled me so much that I lost my balance, and fell backward to the bottom of the stairs.

Immediately, everyone rushed to my side. Grandie held my head in her lap.

"Sabbie!" she shrieked. "Are you all right?"

"Grandma, Grandma, I feel sick. Call the doctor quick, quick, quick! Doctor, Doctor, will I die...?"

"Do you want to?" a dark, unfamiliar voice answered.

Suddenly overwhelmed by this daunting sensation, I opened my eyes and looked around to find out who spoke those words, but saw no one. Instead, I was surrounded by utter darkness, standing completely alone, separated from any other living soul. I blinked numerous times, trying to get my eyes to focus. Still, only pitch-black nothingness closed in on me. I tried calling out for someone, but no sound came out of my mouth. The harder I strained to speak, the more silent I remained. It was as if my mouth was engaging in oral Pilates.

Instinctively, I ran my hands over my belly only to discover that I was no longer pregnant. My babies were gone, and I had no idea what was happening to them or me.

My attempt to start bawling was short-lived, as I could produce neither voice nor tears. Right then I lost all ability to move. When I tried to take a step forward, it was as if my feet were cemented to the ground. I could not move.

Out of nowhere, like the sudden clap of thunder, the noise of barking, snarling vicious dogs resonated in the background. It sounded like a militia was headed in my direction, but I still couldn't see anything. My heartbeat tripled its pace and a wicked spirit of fear gripped me so hard that every nerve in my body went numb. It was so overpowering. I started to tremble.

Oh God, please help me, was all I could think. Almost immediately, I heard a comforting voice, softly assure me that:

"I have not given you a spirit of fear, but of power and love and a sound mind."

"Greater is He that is in you, than he that is in the world."

"I have given you authority over every power of the enemy and nothing shall by any means hurt you."

I took hold of those words and meditated on them repeatedly.

God has not given me the spirit of fear, but He has given me a spirit of power, of love and a sound mind... Greater is He that is in me, than he that is in the world... God has given me authority over every power of the enemy and nothing shall by any means hurt me... God has not given me the spirit of fear...

I must have repeated the scriptures in my head about a hundred times before whatever it was that had attacked me finally let go. My limbs were free to move, and I was finally able to scream. I took off running. Unable to see anything in the darkness, I ran all the same, as fast as my legs would go, until I bumped head-on, into a wall or divider with a small opening.

Without looking back, I walked directly through the opening and wound up in a large, fairly lit hospital room. Six persons dressed in black hooded robes with their backs toward me were huddled about. Relieved to finally be in the presence of others, I briskly walked over to ask for help in finding my babies.

"Excuse me, can somebody please help me?" I called out.

No one responded. I asked again, this time a little louder. They continued to ignore me as though they didn't hear. I wound my way through their assemblage to get a better view of what it was that captured their undivided attention.

To my horror and great amazement, I saw a body that looked exactly like me, bloody and lifeless, on top of a stretcher. The replica also showed no sign of being pregnant and blood was flowing from her abdomen.

"No! Where are my babies?" I shrieked.

The sight sent chills through my body and scared me half to death. Tightly clutching onto my heart, I turned to flee, but the figures around the bed formed an impenetrable barricade. When I looked in their faces, I saw nothing but sinister, glowing eyes, glaring at me. It was then that I realized that these persons were not humans. They were clearly demonic spirits.

"The Blood of Jesus!" I screamed aloud, as they started howling and began closing in on me. I continued to plead the Blood until, one by one, all six of them vanished. Completely exhausted, I sat on the floor, placed my head between my knees, and continued to repeat the words I had spoken earlier.

God has not given me the spirit of fear, but He has given me a spirit of power, of love and a sound mind... Greater is He that is in me, than he that is in the world... God has given me authority over every power of the enemy and nothing shall by any means hurt me...

After what seemed like eons, I felt a light tap on my shoulder. Initially, I was still too frightened to look up, but when I felt it again, I glanced up to see Melvin and Grandie, each holding a newborn baby. At first I wondered if it was really them or two more demonic spirits, but it became apparent when peace immediately flooded my soul.

The darkness had dissipated and pure light emanated everywhere. There was no doorway for the darkness to penetrate. I jumped to my feet, relieved to see my loved ones. I wanted to embrace them, but innately knew I should not.

"Your *dawn* has come, Sabbie," Grandie said, smiling.

"Joy from the Lord is always your strength," followed Melvin.

"Are those *my* babies?" I asked, crying and hoping at the same time.

"The darkest part of the *night* was just *before dawn* came," Grandie said again and handed me the child.

"She's so beautiful!" As I held her in my arms, I heard Melvin repeat:

"Joy from the Lord is always your strength, Sabrina."

I smiled and looked up to see him turn and walk away from me, still holding the other child.

"Wait, Melvin. Can I please hold the baby?" I pleaded.

There was a hint of panic in my voice. He didn't respond and continued walking away.

"It is well, Sabrina. Joy from the Lord is always your strength."

"Why do you keep saying that? Give me my baby. What are you doing?" I stretched forth my hand to reach for him, but to no avail. Melvin kept moving farther and farther away, reiterating the same expression, until he completely disappeared.

Flustered and bewildered. I just stood there in shock. I looked over at Grandie. She just smiled lovingly and said, "It's time."

"Time for what? Why are you doing this to me... you're supposed to love me... Why are you hurting me like this?"

Like clockwork, Grandie too followed after Melvin, but she didn't take the baby I was still holding.

"All is well, Sabrina. Joy from the Lord will always be your strength." She also kept repeating the arcane declaration, until she too finally vanished into the light.

"Please, Grandie. Wait...please, wait..." I stretched forth my hand and reached for her as well, but still to no avail.

)⸺ •)⸺ •)⸺)⸺ •)⸺ •

"Grandie!" I screamed out, but when I opened my eyes she was not there, and neither was my baby girl. Feeling groggy and dazed, I woke up from what felt like a deep sleep, and discovered that I was in a hospital bed.

The sun shone brightly through the massive windowpanes, although raindrops tapped loudly on the glass. The oval clock on the wall indicated that it was a few minutes after ten a.m. The private room resembled the one in the hospital that I had been admitted to the night I found out about my pregnancy. Nerves began to get the best of me, because I knew I wasn't scheduled for delivery for another eight weeks. I had no recollection of what had brought me to this place.

My entire body was in severe pain. Not only did my head hurt like hell, but my arm and stomach did also. Sharp pains cut through my abdomen like lasers. I began to groan loudly and cradle my abdomen. The once huge, firm, protuberance that cradled the twins, was no longer there. My belly was now a soft, jiggling bulge, void of any 'fruit' of the womb. There were huge cuts and scrapes over my arms and legs, and an ace bandage was wrapped tightly over my left wrist. It became clear that I was not wearing any underwear, because I could feel that there was a catheter inserted, and an IV tube protruded from my forearm.

The television mounted on the wall above the foot of the bed was muted and set to the newborn channel. There was no one else in the room with me.

God, please let my children be all right, I silently prayed.

Ten whole minutes passed before Eric finally walked into the room. He stuck his head back out the door and said, "She's awake, Doctor."

"What happened?" I managed to whisper through intense discomfort.

Before he could respond, Dr. Valentine, the one who had diagnosed my pregnancy almost six months ago, walked into the room. I was not expecting to see her.

"Welcome back, Miss Richards," she greeted me. "You gave us a little scare there for a moment. But we're happy to have you back. We really must stop running into each other like this." She chuckled at her own joke.

"According to the report from your husband and the emergency response team, you suffered a mild concussion from the fall you suffered earlier, and it triggered some major contractions and prematurely ruptured some membranes."

"What fall?" I asked. My mind was a complete blank. "What are you talking about?"

She looked to Eric, who then looked at me after Dr. Val gave him a slight nod of approval. He reminded me, ruefully, that as I walked out of his house last night, Monique had angrily charged behind me and kicked me in my back, sending me face forward down his front steps. Dr. Val took over to further explain.

"The impact of the fall resulted in a premature rupture of membranes, which in layman's term, simply means that your amniotic sac broke. Seeing that you were less than thirty-four weeks pregnant, labor presented the possibility of premature complications. The nurses and I tried to do all we could to prevent labor, but too much damage had already been done. In order to prevent further danger to the fetuses, we had to perform an emergency delivery."

I couldn't move. I could barely even think. "Okay, so how did it go?" I inquired, desperately wanting to meet my babies.

Eric turned around to face the window and Dr. Val moved in closer toward me. I knew something was dreadfully wrong.

"Miss Richards, one of the infants did not make it. The fetal monitor transmitted a reading of only one active heartbeat. That was what prompted our team to operate. Your husband signed the consent form, and we admitted you to surgery immediately..."

"My husband?" I interjected, confused. That's when Eric turned to face me. "Oh, okay." That must have been the title he gave himself when he brought me here. The tears began to flow.

The doctor resumed, her voice more solemn. "Although the surgery was a success, we encountered some grave challenges."

The terrified expression on my face prompted her to elaborate.

"There were a few complications during the operation, but we managed to get everything under control without any major calamities."

"What do you mean, 'complications'?" I asked her.

She paused for a second and replied. "You almost died last night, Miss Richards. During the surgery you began seizing, causing your heart rate to accelerate at an abnormal pace. The first female fetus was stillborn upon delivery, but the other was just fine. She's healthy, alert, and looks a lot like her mom." Dr. Val patted me gently on my leg.

I couldn't believe what she was saying. Two babies, two girls, one life. It didn't add up. *My precious, innocent baby.* My heart ached and grieved for my daughter and I couldn't fathom the purpose in all this. *Why, God! Why?*

"Oh, my God. Can I see them?" I asked the doctor.

"Sure, I'll ask the nurse to bring your daughters in right now." She stood, smiled sympathetically at me and left.

"How are you feeling?" Eric asked, once the door was closed.

I couldn't answer, and managed only to shrug my shoulders. I mean, what did he expect me to say? I felt like crap. The pain in my body was overshadowed by the agony in my heart. My baby died last night, for crying out loud. *Our* baby died last night.

"What about you?" I thought to ask him the same.

"I feel low… and responsible… and like I can never forgive myself for what I have put you through. Sabrina, I swear to God that I would understand if you couldn't forgive me either."

"So, where's Monique now?" I asked, surprisingly concerned about her. She was the one primarily responsible for the loss of my daughter and here I was, worried about how she was doing.

"She was arrested, and is being held overnight until the judge can see her in the morning."

"What? Are you serious?"

"Yes. Two officers came to see you earlier to get an official statement from you and me, and to verify whether or not you wanted to press charges. But you weren't conscious. They said they would come back tomorrow, but the doctor told them you were not in a position to deal with any of this right now. She asked them to give you a week to recover. I gave them my statement and they filed a report based on that information. Monique called me earlier and is terrified that you will have her locked up."

"Don't worry, Eric. I'm not going to press any charges against her. She has a son to take care of and regardless of everything she has done to me, I have to let it go."

"That's really big of you, Sabrina, because no one would blame you if you did. You have every right to feel vengeful against her and me, yet you choose not to. I swear to you, Bri, I would never knock you, if you hated both of us for all the hurt that we have put you through. I'm so sorry, Sabrina. I don't think you understand how sorry I am."

Several minutes passed before either of us said another word. Then finally, I broke the silence.

"I'm not angry with you anymore, Eric, and I do forgive you. I forgive both of you." I truly meant it.

He slumped down in the visitor's chair next to the bed, laid his head on my lap, and cried. I mean, he really cried, and of course I couldn't help myself, so I wailed and sobbed right along with him. We grieved for the loss of our daughter, together. Not one word was exchanged between us, but at that moment we knew in our hearts, that in spite of everything, we still loved each other.

Yes, he had cheated on me, and yes, with my best friend *and* got her pregnant. He even contemplated being with her instead of me. In the midst of all that, we pointlessly lost our child. It hurts like hell when I think about it, but the fact still remained. In spite of it all, I *still* loved Eric. But was it enough? How do we pick up all those broken pieces and move on from here?

At this point, only God could do it. There would be so much that would have to change in our lives. We could not go back to business-as-usual. If Eric was truly willing, as he himself admitted, to change his life and live for God, then maybe, just maybe, there was a chance. But no matter what, I promised God that I would not go against His will. As I contemplated the uncertain possibility of our rebuilding a life together, I silently prayed for a sign.

Half an hour passed before two nurses wheeled the children in on plastic rolling carts and parked one on each side of my bed. Taped to the rim of each carriage were pink index cards that read: *Baby Richards* **#1**- *4 lbs 1 oz, Baby Richards #2- 4 lbs 8 oz.*

The nurses left as quickly as they had come, and when the door slammed shut, Eric stirred. Each baby was tightly wrapped in a blanket, and appeared to be sleeping. At first glance I couldn't tell which one was the deceased, until I picked up infant **#1**. I lifted her from the cart and held her close to me.

She was so tiny and pretty, and even though her eyes were closed, I could see that she looked like her daddy. My lips began to quiver, but I held back. Eric reached for the baby, and I handed her to him. He looked adoringly at his dead daughter as the tears rolled down his face.

The excruciating pain in my abdomen throbbed as I leaned over to lift the other baby. She seemed identical to her twin sister, only a little darker in complexion and a bit heavier. I couldn't stop staring at her. Then it hit me, an eerie episode of déjà vu. It was so uncanny. The more I stared at her, the more I realized that I had seen her before, held her before. Eric noticed my bewilderment.

"What's wrong?" he asked, panic coursing through his voice.

"Nothing. Her name is Dawn," I answered, mystified at the revelation.

"Okay. That's nice, I like it. Why..."

"And her name is Joy," I continued in my befuddlement. "Dawn and Joy. My 'Dawn has come.' 'Darkest part of night is just before Dawn.' 'Joy will always be my strength'." I quoted the familiar expressions that popped into the forefront of my mind.

"What are you talking about?" he insisted.

It was all coming back to me now. "Oh, my God! Don't you see? He was trying to tell me! This is what my night episodes were about. They weren't nightmares! They were messages! And they weren't taking her away; they were taking her home. But Dawn is here. My Dawn has come."

Peace and relief flooded my heart. I didn't feel the unbearable anguish anymore. I still felt the hurt over my loss, but the distress was quenched. Eric looked at me as though I were crazy.

"What is going on with you, Sabrina? I know this is hard baby, but you have to keep it together. Our daughter needs you."

"I'm not crazy, you dummy. I just had an epiphany. But you wouldn't understand, so don't worry about it."

"Try me," Eric insisted.

I reminded him of all the dreams I had of Melvin in the past. Eric had been there for most of them.

"Mel wanted to forewarn me of the darkness that would precede the dawn. If you've ever stayed up all night and watched the sky, you would observe that right before day breaks, that's when the night is at its darkest peak. As it is in the natural realm, so it is in the spiritual. The darkness Mel wanted me to be prepared for was everything that transpired between Monique and us, as well as losing Grandie and Joy. But praise God, the dawn was two-fold. Not only have I been reconciled unto Christ, but my mother and I are at peace, and Courtney and I are now better friends than we have ever been. Not to mention the most excellent blessing I could ever dream of; my beautiful daughter, Dawn. She represents a new beginning for me.

"As for what happened during the surgery, I had a really dreadful nightmare, Eric. Only, I don't think it was a dream. I believe it was really happening. You know, I could feel it. I know it sounds crazy, but I could swear the devil was trying to kill me during that operation, maybe even Dawn too. I think that was the reason I underwent those seizure attacks the doctor told me about. This is so bizarre, I know, but I could feel the hand of the devil trying to wipe us out. But God was with me the whole time, reminding me of His Word, and how to use it to ward off the enemy. Thank you God for the Blood of Jesus."

I looked into Eric's face for feedback. "It sounds crazy, right?"

He looked deeply concerned. "Whoa. Yes, it does sound a little out there, but I believe you. It's just that I've never heard of, or experienced anything quite like that before. So then, why did God take Joy in the first place? If He spared Dawn, why not Joy, too?" he asked curiously.

I smiled to myself, knowing exactly what to say. God seemed to work in repeated cycles that resonate in different life circumstances. It was now that I completely understood what Courtney was trying to say when she explained Melvin's sacrifice for Gina. He gave his life to save his mother's; Joy gave her life to save her sister's and mine. And most of all, Jesus' life to save the world.

I explained to Eric that neither of us would have made it through the surgery if Joy had not passed.

"She saved our lives," I told him, the hot tears streaming down my cheeks. "I know this might not mean much to you right now. Trust me, I've been there. But the truth is that our daughter is in a better place, and we are so blessed to still have this beautiful angel right here." I stared lovingly at my precious, sleeping baby.

Eric kissed Joy on the mouth, placed her back in the carriage and gently took Dawn out of my arms. He moved closer to me and kissed my forehead.

"You're right, Sabrina. We are blessed." He stopped talking for a moment and then whispered, "I love you."

I wasn't sure if he was talking to Dawn or to me. I was too exhausted to find out. I just closed my eyes and went back to sleep.

Chapter 21

Dawn and I stayed in the hospital for five days after the surgery. Dr. Val was adamant about not taking any chances by discharging us too soon, as Dawn was a preemie, and I having undergone such a risky operation.

My daughter is the most beautiful thing that I have ever laid my eyes upon. Her eyes, her touch, her smell; everything about her reminds me of God's magnificence. I am sometimes still ashamed of how close I had come to destroying her existence. Whenever I look at her, I can't help but ask for her forgiveness, and can already tell that she's destined to be a woman of great purpose. Next to Jesus, she truly is the best thing that has ever happened to me.

Eric came to the hospital before going to work, returned for his lunch hour, and then stayed until midnight, every day we were there. Visiting hours for dads ended at ten o'clock but the night nurses were lenient and allowed him to stay longer. They said they were so impressed with how doting and attentive he was. "Not very common in today's day and age," they would say. I wonder what they would say if they knew the whole story.

Eric always brought something at every visit; new clothes for me and the baby, toothbrush, toiletries, a new Bible. He was very helpful to me during my recuperation and I wondered if he was the same way with Monique when she had given birth to their son. Probably, it was just Eric's nature to be caring, so I couldn't expect him to be any less attentive to Niqi. When I inquired about her, Eric said he hadn't heard anything further about her case. He said that he had spoken to her the day before, and that she had posted bail. He explained that she was still furious with him, and wouldn't give him any more information as to what was going on with her litigation.

As far as we knew, all seemed to be well, because the police officers never came back to get a statement from me. That was fine. I never wanted her to go to jail anyway. She had a baby to take care of. Even though her sister, Toya, had been helping out during this whole ordeal, still, Gavin needed his mother.

I was determined to trust God that His ultimate will was done in this situation. At the end of the day, that was all I needed.

Before I was sent home, the hospital offered us the option of having a memorial service for Joy in the hospital chapel. We accepted the offer and kept it private, just Dawn and the two of us. There was a Chaplain who gave a small homily in her honor. It was an intimate and moving ceremony and even after the minister left, Eric and I sat with our daughter, who lay lifeless in a doll-size wooden box.

For the first time since I had discovered his indiscretions, I let Eric hold me close to him, and it felt safe. Only God knew what the future held for us as a couple, if anything at all.

)ᑕ •)ᑕ •)ᑕ)ᑕ •)ᑕ •

The day I was discharged from the hospital, Dr. Val came in to sit and talk with me privately. As I prepared to depart, she gave me the update on the baby's condition and mine, and also the Do's and Don'ts of first-time mothering. Tylenol with codeine, a bottle of witch-hazel, and extra gauze were among the medical necessities given to me to ease my recovery.

Dawn, on the other hand, received a bundle of goodies. Two baby bags, ample bottles of formula, Pampers, baby wipes and numerous coupons for other baby products.

After all was said and done, Dr. Val reached in her coat pocket and pulled out a miniature brown plastic bag with a seal usually found on sandwich bags. I looked curiously at it as she handed it to me.

"I believe this belongs to you. The nurse found it when cleaning the room the last time you were here."

At first I thought it was more medication, but my eyes widened as I opened it to see my engagement ring. It was still as beautiful as the first time I had seen it.

Dr. Val continued. "We sent correspondences to the address we had on file, but you never responded. So we decided to lock it up until you came back for it. It looks very expensive, so we figured sooner or later you would come to reclaim it. So here you go. I'm going to ask you to sign something confirming your receipt, okay?"

I exhaled loudly. "Wow, thank you. Believe it or not, Dr. Val, I had no idea it was left here. I really thought Eric had taken it with him."

"Well, I can tell you've been through a lot these past few months. I understand perfectly." She hesitated a bit, then resumed. "May I say something to you, off the record?"

"Sure, anything," I encouraged.

"Listen to me, Miss Richards. I don't know what happened between you and the father of your children, but whatever it is, I know that he loves you. I see couples in and out of here all the time, and most of these men are not half as attentive or even as supportive toward their wives as this young man is toward you."

I looked up from the ring and set my eyes on her. She continued.

"Yes, I know he's not really your husband, but you needed that surgery and he was the only one to consent. Whatever has happened between the two of you, try to let it go. Forgive him and start over. If you still love him, there's still hope for you to share a future along with your daughter. Why go through this alone? Find healing over the loss of your other daughter together. Trust me, it's better to try, and have it not work, than to not try, and regret it for the rest of your life."

"Did Eric say something to you?"

Dr. Val to OR 1 stat! Paging Dr. Val. OR 1 stat!

The loudspeaker interrupted me. Dr. Val patted me on my arm.

"I need to go now. The receptionist has all the paperwork for you to sign before you go. Goodbye, Miss Richards, and take care of yourself and that baby. I hope you'll take my advice."

With that she was gone.

It wound up being Claudia and Silvia who picked us up at the hospital at five-thirty that Friday evening. Eric had stopped by earlier to check on Dawn and me, and to explain that he would not be able to come back for the rest of the day. He had some important business matter to take care of, and would be engaged in some big all-day meeting from which he couldn't be excused. There was no need to worry, because the girls were more than delighted to do it. They brought Dawn to the car while I waited behind to fill out the release forms. Even though I could walk, the attendant who came to see me out insisted that I get in the wheelchair. The pain from the stitches I received was still there, but fortunately, I was able to move about unaccompanied. I tried to protest that it was not necessary, but he was adamant and would not budge until I placed my behind in that chair.

When we arrived in the lobby, I thanked him, got out of the wheelchair and slowly but carefully walked over to the receptionist's desk to sign out. As I stood there, the realization that I still owed the hospital for my last visit suddenly hit me. I was sure that the correspondences they had mailed pertaining to my engagement ring also included the bill. A little embarrassed, I decided to address it first. I handed her my paperwork and waited for her to pull up my account.

Sheila Forbes was the name on the counter.

"Um, Sheila, before you mention it, I want you to know that I am well aware of the fact that I still owe the hospital from my last visit, and can write you a check for the full amount right now."

"What bill are you referring to, Miss Richards? The balance on your last visit was paid in full months ago," she replied.

"Are you sure? How is that possible? There must be some kind of mistake."

She combed through my file and shook her head. "Nope, no mistake here. The entire balance of two thousand three hundred and ten dollars was paid back in December of last year."

"By whom?" I was flabbergasted.

"Ah, let me see." She dabbled on the keyboard of her computer and announced, "Sorry, it was paid in cash."

"You've got to be kidding me."

"Wait, they did sign the receipt, but it's all initials. Maybe you might know."

She turned the monitor toward me and I nearly strained my neck to see it.

E. V. M. was the abbreviated signature. That was all I needed.

After signing all the documents, Sheila informed me that due to the nature of my current admission, I would not be billed for the surgery, delivery, medication or treatment.

When I inquired how that came about, she leaned over and whispered, "Don't ask any questions, and thank your doctor later."

"Okay," I whispered back, "and thank you too. God bless you. Bye."

With that, I was off to meet Claudia and Sylvia, eagerly anticipating embracing the new Dawn in my life.

Chapter 22

The day Dawn and I left the hospital was full of surprises. It all began while we were on our way to my old apartment. Out of nowhere, Claudia said she had to make a quick stop across town before heading home. Admittedly, I was a little irritated by it, only because I wanted to get my baby indoors. But Claudia was doing me a great favor and I had no choice but to get over it.

The look on my face conveyed confusion when her car pulled up in front of Erica and Cameron's brownstone.

"What are we doing here?" I asked, completely clueless. "I didn't know that you knew Erica."

"I don't. Eric called me from his office this morning and asked me to pick up something for you and the baby from here. I don't know his sister at all, and I feel strange going in there. I know it might be a lot to ask, but can you come with me to get it."

"Well, what is it? Do you know?" I was really annoyed now.

"He didn't say. Just that it's something that is necessary for the baby to have. If you want, we can go home, and he can get it himself later."

"No, no, it's okay. I'll go with you." If Eric thought it was so important that it couldn't wait, then I wouldn't be difficult.

"I'll stay with the baby, Sabrina. She'll be fine," Silvia offered.

Every step up to the front door sent ripples of pain through my belly, but I finally made it with Claudia's help. I could really use that wheelchair from the hospital now.

The door was already ajar, so we rang the doorbell to announce ourselves, and walked into the vestibule.

"Come in," someone yelled from the lower level of the house.

"I guess she's expecting you," I proposed to Claudia.

"Yes, I think so too," she said.

As we stepped through the game room of their house, I almost had another seizure attack when what seemed like a multitude of unexpected people burst out screaming, "SURPRISE!!!"

Full of shock and fright, I began screaming and crying simultaneously. This was so unexpected. Eric's parents, Erica, Cameron, Camille, and several other family members and friends were there applauding and ogling me with broad smiles.

The room was decorated in pink and white streamers, ribbons and balloons. There was food and beverages and a big strawberry shortcake in the design of an umbrella, with *Sabrina's Baby Shower* inscribed down the center of it. In front of the fireplace sat a white wicker chair that was adorned with mesh garlands, satin ribbons of various shades of pink and teal, and a money well that stood alongside it. There was a sea of presents surrounding the chair. I was so overcome that I could barely move, much less speak.

"Auntie Sabrina..." Camille came running through the crowd to hug me. "This is for you and my cousin. Are you surprised?" She pulled me over to the chair to have a seat.

"Yes, sweetie. I am very surprised. Where is your Uncle?"

"Over there."

I turned slowly to where she pointed and saw Eric standing at the door, holding Dawn. Courtney, my mother, and Silvia were also with him. I couldn't help but sob some more when Courtney and Gina ran over to hug me.

I was so happy to see them both. How did they pull this off? I was dumbfounded, and had no clue that they were in on this. I had spoken to them both at length after giving birth, and they hadn't mentioned a word. Courtney kept going on and on about how she wished she could have gotten some time off to come to New York, but because it was so close to finals, there was no way her principal would consent to her leaving. Gina talked about how she hated flying, and that I should just hurry and come home so she could take care of me and the baby. They really got me, the little liars.

"Everybody deserves a surprise baby shower," my mother told me. "You didn't think I was going to stay away and not see my first grandbaby right away, did you?"

"When did you guys get here?"

"Last night," they answered in unison.

Courtney continued. "Eric came to get us from the airport and we're checked in at the same hotel as you. All he did was talk about you and the baby."

At the mention of his name, I looked over to see him holding Dawn, making his way through the crowd to show her off. He was so proud of his daughter. I think he felt my eyes burning into him, because instinctively he turned to face me and gave a warm smile. I started to smile back, but just then, Erica ran up to us and gave me a big hug. Courtney and Gina introduced themselves and we engaged in simple small talk about how perfectly the surprise had turned out. The two out-of-towners then excused themselves and went off to mingle with Claudia, Silvia, and some of the other guests.

"Hey there, mama! I can't believe you have a baby now. How does it feel to be a part of the club?" Erica teased.

"To be honest, I'm still in awe. I can't believe she's mine. I'm so thankful." She nodded in empathy. "And thank you so much for all this. I appreciate it more than you can know. I really had no idea." I added.

"Girl, please! This was nothing. That's why it's called a surprise. You aren't supposed to have any idea." Erica paused and looked me up and down. "Are you all right? You look a little pale."

"Me? I'm fine. I'm still in a bit of shock over this whole thing," I chuckled, trying hard to act normal, but still feeling a bit awkward toward her. I think she sensed it too because her next remark confirmed just that.

"You know that I love you, right Sabrina? I always said that Eric could do no better than you, and I still believe that. I'm really very sorry about how badly things turned out between the two of you, and even more so that it has managed to put a rift between us. That's not what I wanted. I love you, and no matter what happens, I want you to know that I'm always here for you and Dawn."

I shook my head agreeably. "I know. Thank you, Erica. I love you too, and I understand that you did what you thought was right. I would be a liar if I said I would have done anything differently had I been in your place. I still want us to remain close friends, especially now that we're family."

"Me too, Bri," she squealed excitedly, threw her arms around me and planted a smooch on my cheek. We both had to laugh. "Listen, we took the liberty of getting your things from the hotel and brought them here. I hope you don't mind. We explained the whole situation to the manager and he wound up charging your card for only the first night."

"Really? That was so nice of you, but I already agreed to stay with my roommate and her sister. I don't want to offend them."

"Well, Eric and I spoke to them about it already and explained that you and the baby would have all the space you need here. They know they are welcome to visit anytime, day or night, and they completely understand. They don't feel bad about it at all, and nothing would make us happier than to have you and Dawn stay here for as long as you want. What do you say?"

"Wow! What can I say, but thanks? But it's only temporary. Dawn and I are going back to Georgia."

She looked surprised. "Really, when?"

"Probably in a couple of days or so. The doctor gave me the okay for her to fly and we'll be going as soon as my body feels up to it."

"Bummer! I didn't realize that Georgia was a permanent arrangement for you. I thought you had stayed away only to clear your head and sort through the issues with Eric."

"Yes. At first it was about all that, but as time went on, I realized that Georgia is my home, and it's where I want to be." I was stunned to hear myself admit it for the first time. I hadn't realized that I had finalized the decision yet, but I guess on a subconscious level, I had already made up my mind.

"I'm sure you've thought about this long and hard, so I won't pressure you. I'll respect your decision, but I don't have to like it." She gave a little chortle and pulled me toward her. "Come here. I'm going to miss you and my niece."

"We're going to miss you too, but you know you guys are always welcome anytime. I haven't discussed it with Eric yet, so please don't say anything."

"I'll stay out of it. Trust me on that."

As we released each other, I excused myself and walked over to talk with Eric's parents for awhile. I didn't want to sit in the chair any longer. I could sense a cramp coming on.

It was such a pleasure to hear how much 'Mom and Dad' adored the baby and they couldn't get over how delightful she was. 'Mom' expressed how much she missed me coming around and offered her condolences on the loss of Joy. She suggested that if I was willing, Eric and I could get through the pain together.

"Won't you forgive him, dear? They're men, and they're fools. It's just their genetic make-up," she said to me. I only nodded and smiled.

Dad was very vocal in admitting that he wasn't worried and was still confident that somehow, someway, Eric and I would work everything out. "I got a lot of money riding on this wedding," he somewhat joked.

I chose not to comment on either of their remarks or to inform them of my decision to move back to Georgia permanently. It was only right that I told Eric before discussing it with anyone else. Subtly, I changed the subject and we chatted for a while about them being grandparents again. That was a favorite topic for Mrs. Morrison. She loved the "grandma" title and played her role very well. She spoiled Camille rotten.

When Dawn started to cry, Eric brought her over to me, and we brought her into another room to be changed and breast-fed. He asked if it was all right for him to stay, and I consented, but only on the condition that he turn away until I was able to get her to latch on. Though he had seen my bare body countless times before, I didn't feel the same ease in just letting it all hang out openly anymore.

The nurses had taught me how to properly get the baby to latch on. I used to think it was easy and natural when I saw other women doing it, but my first few tries were not only frustrating, but also very uncomfortable for both of us. By this time, however, it had become an effortless and a relaxing exercise for both Dawn and me. Eric turned back to us when I was able to properly cover up. He found a place on the bed next to us, and sat.

"She's so beautiful, Sabrina. How did we get so lucky?"

"I don't think luck had anything to do with it, Eric. God is good; that's all I can say to explain it."

"Yeah, you're right. Listen, I've been doing a lot of thinking since our daughter was born, and Sabrina, I really want us to try and work this whole thing out. I still love you so much, and I want us to be a family."

"Eric, I told you already. I can't just make a life decision so rashly as that. God orders my steps now, and besides, you're not even saved, and I cannot be unequally yoked to you. We don't walk side-by-side in the same beliefs."

"Yes, I am saved!" he protested boldly.

"There you go again, thinking this is a joke."

"I'm dead serious, Bri. The other day when we were planning your shower, I was talking to your roommate, Claudia, and I asked her how someone becomes saved. She showed me in the Bible where Jesus died for my sins but through His death and resurrection I could have eternal life. She made me read *Romans 10:9* aloud three times until it came out of my head and got into my heart. *'If you shall confess with your mouth, the Lord Jesus, and shall believe in your heart that God has raised him from the dead, you shall be saved.'* She asked if I was ready to make the decision to accept Jesus into my heart, and I said, 'Yes'. After that, she led me in a prayer, confirming that I was now born again into the kingdom of light, and now I'm saved."

I curiously looked him up and down, waiting with bated breath for him to start laughing and declaring a late April Fools' Day joke. It didn't happen.

I didn't know what to think or believe. Was he for real, or was he doing it because he wanted us to be together again? This was definitely the biggest surprise of the night. I chose to be prudent in my response.

"If you're joking Eric, let me warn you that it's not cool to play with God. But if you're serious, then congratulations are in order. This really is the best decision you will ever make in your life, and I'm really proud of you. But it doesn't mean that we are going to be a couple again. I'm leaving, Eric. I'm moving back to Georgia for good in a few days."

He exhaled loudly and shook his head, greatly disappointed.

"Well, what if I went back with you?"

"That's between you and God. But I don't see how. You have major responsibilities here; your job, family, a house, Gavin. You can't just pick up on a whim to move across the country. These are things you have to pray about and seek God's wisdom. Look, I really wouldn't mind you being close to the baby and me to help play Mr. Mom. Shoot, Courtney and I have plans to go to Jamaica this summer." I tried to add some humor to lighten the tension in the room.

He smiled softly and replied, "You're right. I will pray about it and if a path is cleared to make all those things possible, it means God is allowing it, right?"

"Usually, yes. But if there is no peace about it Eric, don't try to put a square peg in a round hole. It will only be a waste of time and will profit you nothing if you do something that God has not given His blessing for."

"I got you. But I'm not going to give up on us, Sabrina. I love you way too much."

Before I had a chance to respond, someone tapped lightly on the door.

"Come in," I said, carefully trying to remove the now sleeping baby from my chest. She had gone off to dreamland during her parents' conversation. I wrapped her up and placed her between two pillows on the bed.

"Sorry to interrupt, but everybody's looking for you, Sabrina," Claudia reported as she stuck her head in the room. "They want you to come out and open all your gifts."

"Okay, give me a minute. I'll be right there."

Eric got up to leave and I beckoned Claudia to come in. For the next five or so minutes I asked her about the conversation she had with Eric. She confirmed everything he had said, save the fact that he cried like a little boy. She said that it had been a very touching moment and that she honestly believed he was genuine in his intentions.

I had never seen so many presents for just one person. There were bags upon bags of clothes, diapers and wipes, two highchairs, strollers and car seats, a bassinet, a crib, fifteen hundred dollars in gift certificates, numerous trinkets and much more. I didn't know how I would manage to bring them all to Georgia.

Most of the guests left the party at around eight o'clock that evening. Claudia and Silvia helped to clean up the place, then went back to their apartment. I thanked them both for all they had done and promised to go see them before I left New York. Courtney and my mother left a little later than everyone else, and decided to take a cab back to their hotel. They had to fly out to Atlanta the following afternoon.

I also booked a one-way ticket the next day, and returned home four days later.

Chapter 23

Dawn Melissa Morrison was born four pounds and eight ounces, on April 14 at 4:54 a.m.

This honor is presented to proud parents: Sabrina Richards and Eric Morrison.

Congratulations on your little gift from heaven. May all your lives be blessed with love, joy and happiness. We love you.

Your friends, Claudia and Silvia.

I loved reading the crystal plaque the girls had the gift shop make for us. It was by far my favorite gift out of the many Eric and I were inundated with after our daughter's birth. I hung it on the wall in Dawn's new nursery.

After she was born, Gina and Courtney had invited a few friends from church to come together to convert Melvin's old room into a nursery. They thought it was time to move out all his clothes, shoes and other memorabilia, and put the room to good use. I agreed. It was time to move on.

We donated most of his things to the shelter outreach ministry, but kept his accolades and trophies, placing some in the living room curio and others in my room.

Courtney also opted to keep a few. It worked well that way, because we were all still able to keep his memory alive, while still accepting and acknowledging that he was gone. It was a big, but very necessary step for me, and as always, God's peace gave me the strength that I needed.

When I had returned to Georgia almost three months ago, I was surprised and delighted to see Dawn's new room. It hardly looked like the boys' room it had been before. The walls were painted sky blue with clouds, rainbows and sun-showers, with cute cuddly bears bouncing on the rainbows. And each of the three windows was adorned with silk-blend pink and blue curtains. The theme looked like the Care-Bears, my favorite cartoon characters growing up. Gina and Courtney had really outdone themselves, and I was so touched.

Several unopened gifts and cards were lined up against the wall, just waiting to be unwrapped. God had blessed us with so much. I now clearly understood when He promised in His Word that He would open up the windows of heaven and pour out blessings beyond our capacity to contain them. It was true. These gifts overflowed our space, and there was so much more still to come.

Before we left, Eric assured me that he would hire a moving or delivery company to transport all the big gifts from Erica's home in New York to mine in Georgia. Since there was no rush, I told him he could take his time. Even at two and a half months old, Dawn was still so small, and not yet ready for a crib. She hardly slept during the night hours, so for now I kept her in the bed, snug and secure, next to me. The only large item I took with me was one of the two-in-one baby carriages we received, which had been convenient for transporting Dawn through the airport the day we came home.

Not a day went by that Dawn's father hadn't called to check up on us. He constantly whined about how much he missed her and wanted to be closer to his daughter. He told me that he had not given up on God making a way for him and me. Almost every time we spoke, he would ask me whether or not I still loved him.

I told him that I didn't think I could ever stop, but we would need more than just love to make a relationship work between us again. God has to be the Alpha and the Omega in any relationship I entered into ever again. All he would say was, "If you still love me, that's all I need to know."

Eric was very focused when it came to Dawn. He wanted to know everything, even the minor details about all of her medical visits, down to the pediatrician's comments after her weekly examinations.

I expressed how heartrending it was for me to watch her get that first immunization shot. She cried and screamed as if she was being slaughtered. I had to stop myself from crying right along with her. At one point, I was tempted to turn the needle on the nurse, just to see how she would like it, but I understood that the painful procedure was a necessary evil.

Night Before Dawn

Because of Dawn's reaction to the pain, her father insisted that I wait until she was a little older before piercing her ears. I personally thought it was better to get it over and done with while she was still so young, but I conceded to respect his wishes. I agreed to wait until she was six months old.

Dawn was growing so fast and all she did was eat, poop and sleep. At two months she gained a whopping three pounds, putting her at seven pounds eight ounces. Her doctors were thoroughly pleased with her progress, and needless to mention, so were mom and dad.

Being a single parent with such a young infant was extremely difficult, and I thanked God daily for my mother. She was such a pillar of support to Dawn and me. She undertook some of the night-feeding sessions, which was such a blessing to me, because sometimes I was just too tired to get up. I mean, the baby would sleep maybe forty minutes at a time before waking up to eat or to be changed.

I would leave ample bottles of formula and breast milk in the fridge for her convenience. It was really very taxing, but my mother came in, rolled up her sleeves and took over for me many a night. Sometimes Courtney would come to do a shift also, usually on the weekend.

I'm almost sure that it was for this very reason that God ordained it that man and woman should raise a family together. Lately, a lot of my prayer time was spent asking

Him to somehow, in some way, grant my desire for a husband, be it Eric or someone else.

☾☽ ☾☽ • ☾☽ • ☾☽ ☾☽ •

Gina and Courtney went to great lengths regarding the planning of Dawn's Christening. They rented a large section of Miccelino's, a popular Italian restaurant in College Park, and invited almost the whole neighborhood. Invitations were also extended to Eric's family and our friends in New York. I hardly lifted a finger to participate in the preparations. My only request was that the cake have a picture of Dawn decorated on it. Yes, I was one proud mama!

On the Saturday morning, a week before the baby's Christening, Gina and Courtney went to the party store to get decorations and favors for the invited guests. Dawn and I stayed home. At a little after one o'clock, the doorbell rang. The baby was taking her afternoon nap and I wanted to get the door before it rang again. I figured it was Gina and Courtney needing help with the packages they purchased. They had done the same thing the day before when they went to pick up groceries for the house, and woke the baby in the process. Somewhat exasperated, I scurried to unlock the door and admonish them.

"Could you guys please just call me the next time…"

I stopped in mid-sentence when I opened the door to see Eric Morrison standing there. An 18-foot U-Haul truck was parked in front of the house. I gasped loudly, totally bowled over to see him.

Right then I became conscious of my appearance. I looked like a fright, with my hair totally disheveled and uncombed. I had on an old, tattered velour sweat suit, and now it struck me that I hadn't taken a shower since the day began.

"Oh, snap! What are you doing here?" I asked nervously, my heart racing out of control. "The Christening is not till next week Saturday. Did you get the dates mixed up?"

"No. I thought I would surprise you and bring the baby's gifts." He was very cheery and upbeat. "You still look good, even when you're bumming, you know that?"

"Shut up!" I couldn't help but smile.

"Can I get a hug?"

I gave a quick embrace and invited him inside.

"Where is everybody?" he continued to ask, as I led the way into the living room.

"Mom and Court went to get some favors for the party, and the little princess is resting. She just went down for her afternoon nap."

"Can I look in on her?"

"Sure, but please don't wake her, Eric. She'll be up all day after that."

He promised not to, and I directed him to my room. While he was upstairs, I ran to the powder room to pin my hair in a clip and make sure that my face was at least clean. He was gone for about fifteen minutes. When he returned to the family room, I had two glasses of iced tea in a tray set on the coffee table. He took a seat on the couch and I sat on the ottoman across from him.

"She's getting so big and beautiful, just like her mom," he commented as he sat.

I smiled coyly and pretended not to hear the last part of his remark. "Yes, the girl can eat."

The silly smile lingered on my face and I pointed to the tray with the glasses to divert any attention away from me.

"I thought you might want something to drink. It's your favorite."

"You remembered. Thank you," he replied, reaching for his drink.

"Oh, don't be silly, Eric," I scoffed at him.

It felt so surreal to have him in my home, outside of New York. He still looked good to me, in his white tee, blue jeans, and blue-and-white sneakers. He looked so happy, like he didn't have a care in the world. I had missed him since the last time we were together, and despite how I looked, I was glad he came. Neither of us said anything more for about two long minutes. Then eventually we both started talking at once.

"So how was your..."

"I have some big..."

I apologized and insisted that he go first.

"Okay. I have some really big news to tell you."

I nodded eagerly, urging him to continue.

"Well, Sabrina, the U-Haul that's outside your house doesn't just hold the baby's things alone. Inside are also most of my furniture and other personal belongings."

He pulled out a piece of paper from his back pocket and handed it to me. It was a real estate description sheet. I took it from him and read it carefully. It was a listing of a house for sale, located at 7 Millstone Place, which was only a few houses up the street from ours.

"Okay..." I said cynically, waiting for further clarification.   "I just bought it!" he blurted out gleefully.

"What did you say?"

"You heard me. I just bought that house at the top of Millstone. All right, let me explain. Comstock has just built a new division in the Atlanta office, and they needed a couple of Executive Directors from the New York office to volunteer for a special relocation assignment. They proposed an offer that I thought was too good to pass up. A twenty-thousand-dollar sign-on bonus, plus relocation and rental assistance, and a company car. But the position is only for one year. You know how I feel about renting, and I figured the money that would be wasted could be put to better use in a mortgage. So I decided to invest in some property here. I found a realtor, who found me this place. It was totally coincidental that it was the same street as yours, and I thought it was a sign from God. So I bought it. What do you think?"

Are you out of your mind, was what I thought. Was this really God's doing? I was partly glad and partly wary. I didn't want to put too much emotion into my response.

"Wow. I don't know what to think, Eric. Are you sure that you are doing the right thing? What about your house in New York?"

"It's being rented."

"Well, what about Gavin, your son? I'm sure this decision didn't go over well with Monique."

"Gavin is fine. Monique and I are in the process of working out a formal visitation schedule and besides, she is seeing someone new now."

I laughed out loud. "Really? Why am I not surprised? Some people never change. Who is it this time, your father?"

He didn't laugh at my joke. "Not funny. No, she's actually dating her lawyer."

The bewilderment that shot across my face urged him to continue.

"I found out that even though you didn't press any criminal charges against her, the District Attorney's office did. Apparently the police came back to the hospital to speak with you, but you had already been released by then. They spoke at length with your doctor, who gave them the details of your injuries and cause of Joy's death. Apparently they had enough information to proceed in bringing a case against her without your actual statement. Monique was able to find a lawyer to defend her case, and it wound up being much more than just a client-counselor relationship."

"Oh, man, I feel so bad for her. I didn't realize that the incident was still an issue. I sure hope it all works out in her favor. But you must be so overcome with jealousy that Niqi has a new boyfriend?" I said facetiously.

Eric rose from the couch and knelt before the ottoman.

"Oh, please Sabrina. I don't care about what Monique does. She's Gavin's mother, and I'll always love and be there for my son. Monique and I were a momentous mistake. I wish that I could turn back the hands of time to change what happened, but I can't. Sabrina, I miss you so much! You're all I think about. I need you in my life and I can't go on living from day to day knowing that you'll never be in my arms again. I miss you so much, baby," he sensuously whispered, and slid his body upward, planting a passionate kiss on my lips.

Electricity and powerful chemical surges shot through every cell and artery in my body. I got weak in the knees, even though I was still sitting down.

"Please, don't do that again," I whispered, barely able to even speak.

"Don't fight it; you know you feel it too." He tried to kiss me again, and it took all my strength to resist him. I rose up quickly from my seat, but was hardly able to stand.

"Why are you doing this? You can't just run in and out of my life, break my heart, and expect to pick up right where we left off, just because you had a change of heart."

"It's more than just a mere change of heart, Sabrina. I was a fool to betray you. I can clearly see that, and now I've come to my senses."

"*You've come to your senses,*" I echoed. "You hurt me so deeply, and now you expect me to simply forget and give you my whole heart without reservation, all over again. Just like that? God asks us to forgive. I don't yet know how to forget, Eric. How do I know that you won't *lose* your senses again? What is my guarantee? There is none. You're asking me to take a big risk that you might not hurt me again, based on your word, and it's not fair for you to expect that much from me."

I spoke with great vigor and resolution, and I meant every word of it.

"I know it's a lot. But Bri, like you said before, God is now the foundation and the basis we can build on. I have not stopped praying about this since you and Dawn left New York. I truly believe He's giving me a second chance with you, and now I'm here to ask you for that chance. Let me love you the right way. Let me honor and cherish you the way you deserve. Let me be the one you love, and the one to love you. Sabrina, allow me the honor of spending the rest of my days filling your life with sunshine."

He quoted the familiar lines he used the night he proposed to me in Negril, and my heart was beginning to soften after every word he spoke. He still had his hold on me.

"I'm not denying that I still love you, Eric, because I do, very much. But it's not going to be that simple. You're going to have to work like hell for my heart, because it doesn't come cheap. Do you understand me?"

He remained on his knees, and wrapped his arms around my legs.

"I'll do anything, go anywhere, to win your heart back, Sabrina. As God is my witness, you're the only woman I'll ever want, and with you is where I want to be. I love you, Sabrina. I love you... I love only you. Please give me one last chance to show you how much. Please."

He begged so well that it broke my heart. I loved him too and wanted to grow old with him. That was all I ever wanted, ever since the first time he approached me at the bar counter at Klub Elektrik, almost six years ago. I knelt down to meet him face to face, with tears in my eyes.

"All right." I surrendered willingly.

He looked at me in disbelief. "'All right?' Does that mean yes?"

"It means that I want to try. I love you too, Eric. I never stopped and I'm willing to see what God has in store for us, but the only way this can work is if we do it His way. Okay? That means it can't be like how it was when we first started. We have to do all things virtuously and honorably in His sight."

"For Him saving me and giving me you, I'll do anything God asks me to do from now on. Anything, and that's my promise to Him." Still on our knees, he hugged me close to him and looked heavenward, tears rolling down his cheeks.

"Thank you, Jesus, for giving me this chance. With it I promise to honor You, and Sabrina, and our children for all the days of my life. I promise."

"You're crazy," I chuckled, tears of joy also streaming down my face. "You better believe He's going to cash in on that vow someday. I hope you really understand what you just did."

"I do." He replied with absolute conviction.

As we both stood up, the shrill cries of our daughter came blaring from upstairs. I wiped my tears, picked up the remote control to turn on the television, and plopped myself down on the couch. Eric looked at me curiously.

"What?" I exclaimed. "You better go and get your daughter. And get used to it sweetheart, because I'm on my way...going away, for many a day. Yes, sir, Courtney and I are going to Jamaica!"

Dear Reader,

If any part of this story has touched your heart and you have not yet accepted Jesus Christ as your personal Lord and Savior, I invite you now to do so. If you too are searching for truth, salvation and restoration, I encourage you to repeat [out loud so the devil can hear you!] the same sinners' prayer that Sabrina confessed.

> *"Lord Jesus, I recognize that I am a sinner and that I need a Savior to save me from my sins. I believe that You died on the cross to redeem me from the curse of sin and death. Today I confess with my mouth and believe in my heart that God raised You from the dead. Come into my heart and abide; I choose you to be the Lord of my life, now and forevermore. In Jesus' name I pray, amen."*

If you have prayed the above prayer in faith, I congratulate you on this awesome decision! You are now born-again, a new creature in Christ Jesus and I welcome you into the family of God. It's really that simple.

Now that you are a Christian, I encourage you to get a copy of the Bible and find a sound Bible-teaching church so that you can grow in your new relationship with Christ.

Feel free to send me an email or visit my site to share your testimony of what the Lord has done in your life. May God's love, grace and blessings continue to abound toward you as you go forth in the plans and purposes He has for your life.

Yours in Him,

Roschelle McKenzie

For comments, feedback and/or additional book orders, please visit the author's website: www.readywriteriam.com

Or email the author at: readywriteriam@gmail.com

Night Before Dawn

A Novel

ROSCHELLE MCKENZIE

True Vine Publishing
P.O. Box 22448
Nashville, TN 37202

www.TrueVinePublishing.org